The Narzat

The Narzat

Luke Marchant

Illustrated by Rory Walker

Published in the UK in 2024 by Everything with Words Limited,
Fifth Floor, 30–31 Furnival Street, London EC4A 1JQ

www.everythingwithwords.com

Text copyright © Luke Marchant 2024
Illustrations © Rory Walker 2024

Printed and bound in Great Britain by
CPI Group (UK) Ltd, Croydon CR0 4YY

A CIP catalogue record for this book
is available from the British Library.

ISBN 978-1-911427-384

For Seth, my Narzat

Chapter 1

The Jumble Jungle Wood

The Jumble Jungle Wood is **VERY** far away.

Of course, when I say *very*, I mean ridiculously, incredibly, unbelievably, mind-bogglingly far away. Imagine the longest walk you've ever been on – one where the adults looked a bit lost and started snapping at each other. One where you were worrying your feet would drop off, or that you would have to eat one of your parents in order to survive. Well, multiply that walk by the biggest number you can think of and you start to grasp how far away the Jumble Jungle Wood truly is.

To get there, you have to stumble through the coldest parts of icy wastelands, push past where the

North and South Winds meet, hot foot it across the Hooha Desert, and wade for days through the Mosquito Marshes of Swampland. You'll have to be silent when you sail across one ocean (to avoid angry pirates) and be extra loud when crossing the next (to scare off cowardly pirates). You have to take many right turns, and even more wrong turns. Sometimes you'll have to crawl, sometimes you'll have to sprint, and sometimes you'll even have to do both. If you can do all of this (and put up with a lack of food, sleep, comfort, or clean socks) you might just reach the feet of the Three-Headed Mountain. And if you

can bear to cross that, then – finally, at last! – you'll have reached the Jumble Jungle Wood.

And, oh my goodness, it is worth every step of the journey.

The Jumble Jungle Wood is a place like no other. It is filled with wildlife from your wildest dreams, and awash with creatures from beyond your imagination. From the moment the sun rises over the Three-Headed Mountain, the trees quiver with sweet snarls and howling hoots, like an orchestra of a thousand fascinated conversations. The ground is a riot of colour – from the tropical petals of the *rainbow rose* to the flashing feathers of the *coo-ee-parrot* – and a hundred scents fill the air. About eighty two of them are wonderful, ten of them are unusual and eight of them are just dreadfully smelly.

As you wander through the jungle – and I hope you do one day – the first things that will cause your jaw to drop will be the trees. Not just because they are amazing but because they are so different. *Towering toombas* loom proudly, covering the sky with a leafy green ceiling. Their bases are hugged by *cuddle-shrubs*, whilst *twirly twiglets* float on by. In some areas, *sobbing saplings* droop over flowing rivers (their blue leaves resemble giant teardrops) whilst *choco-oaks* drop vast swathes of sweeties onto the forest floor. In some places, *upside-down trees* dominate the ground and their roots swirl above them, and, in others, *shy hawthorns* try to hide behind each other.

It is said that if you chop a tree down, you can count its rings to see just how old it is. Not only is this especially time consuming, but you also end up losing a tree. Fortunately, in the Jumble Jungle Wood, you just need to look at a tree to know its age. The oldest trees look wistfully to the sunset and moan in the wind about how the youthful shrubs of today are behaving, whilst baby bushes cuddle to their nearest parent. And teenage trees stand apart from the rest with their branches stuck in their pockets, mumbling something about being embarrassed.

As you have probably guessed, there are many spectacular creatures in the Jumble Jungle Wood. The sheer number of species, the incredible difference between each animal, the way each creature has adapted to its habitat – every single member of the jungle is a dazzling marvel who I could tell you about for twenty pages or more. However, there is one particular animal – or should I say beast? – that makes every other pale in comparison. It is unique in every possible way and special in all the others. It's worth travelling to the Jumble Jungle Wood just to see it. Prepare yourself to meet...

THE NARZAT!

Chapter 2

The Narzat

If you combined the muddiest puddle with a dustbin full of dirt, you still wouldn't have something as grimy as the Narzat. From head to toe, he is covered in muck from a hundred different adventures. Leaves litter his matted hair, and sludge oozes between his toes. In fact, both of his feet are so dirty that he has developed a protective layer of muck under his soles, which means he can traipse over any terrain with barely a wince.

If you were to stand back to back with the Narzat, you would probably be a little bit taller (or he would be a little bit shorter). Either way, you wouldn't want to stand next to him for too long for fear that you'd get Narzat muck on your clothes.

It's hard to describe the Narzat's true shape, as bits of leaf, bush and the occasional bug have all stuck to his body making him look like a badly drawn shrub. It would be easy to mistake him for a plant if he weren't charging around all the time, wind-milling his arms and stamping his happy feet.

Besides the muck, three other things stand out about the Narzat:

1. **His grin.** He has the biggest, toothiest, yellowest smile that you have ever seen. It says hello and goodbye all at the same time, and glows with the warmth of someone who just wants to be friends.

2. **His eyes**. His eyes are of the deepest brown. This brown is unlike the muddy stains surrounding his body – it is a brown of the deepest earth, a brown that somehow manages to catch the light and twinkle. There is nothing warmer than the flash of the

Narzat's eyes paired with the shine of his smile.

3. **His 'shiny'**. It is unusual for any creature to wear jewellery, but the Narzat is not your usual creature. Around his neck is a sparkling silver chain, and from that chain hangs a sparkling silver locket. He is not sure how long he has owned the shiny – it's just always been there. The Narzat's 'shiny' is the only thing that he ever cleans.

As I hope you have gathered, the Narzat is both friendly and foul, both smiley and smelly. Many creatures in the Jumble Jungle Wood overlook his peculiar appearance and even more peculiar odour and enjoy the fun of his games and the warmth of his friendship. Indeed, even though the Narzat only talks in gravelly grunts and hoots and howls, there is some wonderful music about his laughter that brings you closer.

Sadly, the Narzat didn't always enjoy friendship in the Jumble Jungle Wood. In fact, there was a time when he had no friends, chums, pals or even mates at all! What a sad and lonely time that was for the poor fellow. He would stumble across the forest floor, lean against the sobbing saplings, and slowly kick his way through muddy puddles. Occasionally, he tried to play games that weren't half as fun on your own, such as catch, or jungle badminton. He walked to the murkiest swamps to the feet of the Three Headed Mountain, looking for someone to talk to.

It was one special night that he sat on a particularly uncomfortable rock (the rock later turned out to be a particularly uncomfortable tortoise – you'd be uncomfortable too with a Narzat sat on you) and looked up at the stars. His brown eyes brimmed with tears and he clutched his shiny with one hand. On the pendant were etched delicate words, which glinted in the blueness of the moon. The Narzat read them slowly, mouthing the words. Soft words. Special words. I'm not sure if he knew what they meant, but he certainly knew what they felt.

The locket said:

When the night is long and dark,
We fear the sun shall not rise.

But, oh! My love! Soon it does,
And what beauty fills our eyes!

The Narzat clutched the shiny extra hard and made a special wish, for a friend. Any friend would do.

Some of you may believe in the power of wishes, and some of you may just believe in coincidences, but it may please you to know that the very next day the Narzat met not just one friend, but two friends. And they were the two very best friends that he could have ever hoped for.

Chapter 3

The Narzat's Friends

The next morning, the Narzat was rustling up a fine breakfast of *shnonkberries* and *square-pear*. The former is very easy to eat, but unbearably sour whilst the latter – a large cube of fruit – is wonderfully sweet but as difficult to eat as any other cube. Fortunately, the Narzat enjoyed the best of both fruits and the forest was filled with the soft chewing and grunts of glee that only he could produce. That is when a noise interrupted him.

"Oh! I say – are you eating shnonkberries? They're bizarre aren't they!" cried a voice from behind.

The Narzat whirled round, dropping his square-pear – but all that faced him was the pink bark of the surrounding trees.

"Ooh! square-pear as well!" the voice continued. It was a happy voice that seemed to speed along like a merry stream. "You know that it's grown in the wrong shape? It's supposed to be shaped like a pear. Which means it's gone wrong. You could say it's gone pear-shaped, although it isn't pear-shaped is it? Hmm…"

A feather of the darkest blue slowly wove its way through the air, catching the Narzat's eye.

"Oh no! Can't believe I've lost one of those now – you know what they say… 'Hair today, gone tomorrow!' Hahaha…except it's not hair – it's a feather. But are they the same? I'm not too sure…"

The voice carried on babbling away as the Narzat raised his head. Hanging above him, upside down and chuntering away, was the most exquisitely beautiful bird he had ever seen. Almost all of its feathers were of the darkest blue – the colour of a still ocean at midnight – and it spread its wings so they could shimmer in the morning light. Its legs were striped neatly with white and black, and a pair of wide bulging eyes sat neatly either side of a long, curved beak, which resembled a floating banana. Atop of the bird's head, and protruding from its tail were even more feathers. They stood proudly on end and shone with each colour of the rainbow. The Narzat gasped in delight and a smile leapt across his face.

"I do apologise! I must introduce myself!" chortled the bird, flapping his wings. He let go of the tree branch and... well, I'd like to say he flew gracefully to the floor. Instead he fell, fluttering wildly, and with a loud squawk. Bouncing off the forest floor, he brushed himself off and extended a wing.

"I am the Chatty Chirper Bird! But you can just call me Chatty Chirper. We're a wonderful species... we're not very good at that whole flying malarkey, but boy can we fall with style!"

The Narzat happily shook the Chirper by the

wing, and they started walking together, talking all the way. It was the most enjoyable conversation that either of them had ever had – the Narzat loved to listen and the Chatty Chirper loved to... well... chat. The Narzat scampered along, occasionally dropping to his hands to crawl, whilst the Chirper lolloped and stumbled alongside him.

They walked for the best part of a day, sharing laughter and smiles, watching as happy moments turned into happy hours. So engrossed were they in this growing friendship that neither of them had noticed how the forest had suddenly grown a little darker, the trees had grown a little unfriendlier, and the noises had grown a whole lot creepier. Had they only been a little more focused, had they only looked round a little more, had they only realised how the sun seemed to be hidden by a ceiling of thorny leaves, they would have realised that they had ended up in the Deep Dark Depths.

If you ever go to the Jumble Jungle Wood, it is worth you remembering that the whole place is full of wonder and joy – as long as you stay clear of the Deep Dark Depths. It is a place full of teeth and claws, a place where the most beastly of beasts lurk and await. It is said that the worst noise you could ever hear in the Deep Dark Depths is silence, because that means something truly horrible is heading along. It is a shame that the Chatty Chirper was too busy talking to notice how eerily silent the place was around him.

"And my seventeenth favourite type of rain is the warm, drizzly drops that you get every Sunday in the warm swamps! Or is that my eighteenth?" prattled the bird. "But I also have to – ow! Ow!"

Something had slammed into the Chirper's foot, and something else had slammed into his shin.

The Narzat, upset that his new friend had been hurt, reached down, scooped up the mysterious cause of pain, and held it in front of him.

Standing in his palm, looking mightily miffed, was a tiny green lizard. Her slender body moved and curved like water. You could almost be forgiven for thinking that she was a snake, were it not for her four narrow legs, each adorned with four narrow toes. As the Narzat look at her, he was struck by how wonderfully expressive her face was. Thin black eyebrows danced across her forehead like exclamation marks on a page. Beneath them, a pair of wide eyes shone with a vibrant yellow; beneath her eyes two nostrils flared and, beneath them, a tight-lipped mouth stretched from ear to ear. The mouth seemed to twitch at the corners, being both a smile of *Hello!* And a frown of *Who are you?* Her whole body was of the brightest emerald green, except for the beautiful blue patterns that spiralled down her spine.

Raising herself onto her hind legs, the lizard raised two hands (or should I say feet?) and started to gesture wildly. Her fingers (or should I say toes?) danced nimbly, and she began to mime many marvellous gestures at speed. All the while, she scowled and pointed furiously into the forest.

"Oh! I know what you are! You're a Looky Lizard!" cried the Chatty Chirper.

Yes! nodded the Looky Lizard in exasperation. Of course she did not say this out loud, but gestured quite emphatically.

"They're marvellous creatures, these lizards!" continued the bird proudly. "They have no voice but boy can they talk! They speak all kinds of sign language, mime, Makaton and more! I've thought of learning some myself but I can't stay quiet for that long!"

The Narzat was only half listening to his feathered friend for the Looky Lizard was growing more and more animated in his palm. He wished he could understand what she was saying, but her gestures – so rapid and lyrical – left him confused.

So when she waved her arms in a way that said: *You've got to run! It's not safe!*

The Narzat just frowned.

When she mimed: *Please! Go! There's no time!*

The Narzat just raised an eyebrow.

"I didn't know there were many of these left!" continued Chirper. "I'd heard they'd all been eaten by a herd of Ravenoserous – or is it Ravenoserouses? Or Ravensoer – i? *Anyway*, it's marvellous to meet a real – Ow!"

The Looky Lizard leapt over, wrapped one arm around the Chirpers beak and made a shushing gesture with the other. When she was certain that the bird would be absolutely quiet, she slowly released his beak and dropped to the ground.

Raising herself up, she fearfully glanced over her shoulder and lifted one, scaly finger.

"Um… one?" inquired the Chirper.

The Looky Lizard cradled her head in her hand, and rolled her hands forward in a way that said: *Come on, birdbrain. Think about what I'm saying…*

"Ooh! One word! One word! You want me to guess one word! I played a game like this at my Aunty's a few summers ago, before the Great Wave separated us all and…"

He was silenced by the Narzat slowly reaching across and holding his beak. The Lizard shot a look of thanks and tried her best mime yet. Opening her mouth, and pulling her angriest face, she showed all of her teeth. She made claws with her hands and puffed out her chest, trying to look as ferocious as possible.

"A scary creature? Let's see…" guessed the Chirper.

"Is it a *tigergator*?"

No, shook the Looky Lizard.

"A *fangdoodle*? A *grunket*? The Six Horned Chargemeleon?"

The Lizard shook her head despairingly.

"Or is it… "

A roar burst through the jungle, interrupting the Chirper. The roar boomed with anger, and the trees shuddered at its sound.

"Oh my! That sounds like the Ravenoserous… Ooh! Is it Ravenoserous? Is that the word!"

The Looky Lizard's whole body nodded, although she did raise an eyebrow in a way that said… *Finally, you nitwit*.

She pointed into the jungle.

"Ravenoserous… over… there?" gulped the Chirper.

But the time for guessing games had been and gone. The thunder of hungry footsteps seemed to be stomping closer to them, shaking the ground. The roar – that terrible, booming roar – sounded again and this time it was oh so much nearer.

It's not clear who grabbed who first, but the Narzat, the Chatty Chirper and the Looky Lizard found themselves running together, holding hands and wings, as the footsteps followed them deeper into the Deep Dark Depths…

Chapter Four

Running from the Ravenoserous

The Ravenoserous is always hungry. It has far too many stomachs, and not enough time to fill them. For this very reason, it is perhaps one of the most ill-tempered beasts that you will ever encounter. Except, I really hope you don't encounter one.

The Ravenoserous is a hideous ball of muscle, and claws and teeth. Coarse, white fur lines its body whilst black dots are littered across it like splashes of ink. Its broad shoulders and broad hips are only matched by its broad stomach, whilst its muscular legs hold it high off the ground. Its gigantic feet are draped with more claws than are needed – every thundering footstep the Ravenoserous makes is worsened by the sound of the snickety-snack of its razor-sharp toe nails. Of course, the most horrific thing about the Ravenoserous is its jaws. The creature can open its mouth so wide that it could feasibly swallow its own head. Within these jaws are rows, upon rows upon rows of jagged teeth. The rows seem to go on forever so it wouldn't be surprising if the Ravenoserous even had teeth inside all of its stomachs! In fact, some people even claim that the Ravenoserous has teeth on its eyelids but this is probably nonsense – no one could ever get close enough to look a Ravenoserous in the eye without being gobbled up.

As the Narzat sprinted with his friends, he threw a look back over his shoulder. This was probably the first time he had ever seen something that he did not want to be friends with (a strange occurrence that would only ever happen to him twice). The Ravenoserous charged with the speed of a nightmare, and the Narzat felt his heart race almost as fast as his feet.

The Looky Lizard tugged on his hand and pointed to a group of approaching rocks. She waved her hands urgently, and the Narzat found that he could almost understand what she meant.

Hide. There.

The Chatty Chirper was undergoing a strange sensation. For once in his life, he was lost for words. This did not mean he remained silent, but rather he just burbled away with a series of terrified noises.

"Glar! Bar! Mango pants! Yarpety yarpety yarg!" he squawked, whilst flapping his wings in panic. Of course, the flapping only managed to lift him a leaf's length above the ground as he sprinted.

The three friends reached the rocks. There were two particularly large boulders, littered with purple pebbles on top. They dived behind them, stopping to pant heavily. The Narzat glanced around the corner of the stones and realised a rather horrible thought. It was a thought so unpleasant that he rather it had remained *un*thought, but sadly he could not *un*think it.

The Ravenoserous was still heading towards the rocks.

It may have been a giant, hungry monster, but it was not stupid. It was going to leap at the rocks and find them. The Narzat glanced at his friends – the

Chatty Chirper was still babbling in terror and the Looky Lizard was covering her eyes in silent horror. These were his friends. And they were going to be gobbled.

Before I tell you what the Narzat did next, it is probably worth me mentioning something about him that you may not have realised. He is incredibly brave.

Diving from behind the rocks, the Narzat beat his chest and widened his eyes, letting out the loudest roar that he could.

The Ravenoserous stopped in its track. It had eaten many things. Indeed, it had roared at many things... but nothing had ever roared back.

The Narzat did not leave the Ravenoserous much time to think. He then decided to sprint away from the rocks, leading the creature away from his friends. If the Narzat was running anywhere else in the Jumble Jungle Wood, he might have stood a chance. Sadly, this was the Deep Dark Depths, a place where every creature and animal seeks to cause you harm. It was as he was running that a sneaky vine snaked its way out from a tree and tripped him up.

He stumbled, tumbled and fell, before trying to fumble to his feet. I say trying because the

Ravenoserous was upon him. It placed a mighty paw on the Narzat's chest, forcing him down. It leaned forward – toothy eyelids fluttering – and widened those terrible jaws. Rank, hot breath blasted from its many stomachs as it leaned forward for a final bite.

Ping!

A purple blur struck the Ravenoserous painfully on the back of the ear. It leapt up, releasing the Narzat.

Ping!

Another purple blur struck the Ravenoserous again, this time on the bottom.

It whirled round, fury crumpling its face, before another purple blur struck it on the nose.

The Looky Lizard was standing on top of the rocky boulders, flinging purple pebbles at the monster with all of her might. The great brute roared and charged towards her. Food had always run away from the Ravenoserous, but now it was roaring and fighting back?

"Oh! No! Yoo-hoo! Ravenoserous! I say – look over here!" cried a voice.

Inches away from the Lizard, the Ravenoserous stopped and turned. Climbing up a tree and waving was the Chatty Chirper.

"You don't want to eat her – she's barely a snack. I, on the other hand, am particularly succulent and I should imagine that I'd probably taste beautiful with a touch of garlic ..." continued the bird. Cowardly though he was, he could not bear the thought of his friends being eaten either. He might not be able to roar or fight, but could he chatter!

The sound of roasted garlic Chirper was too appealing to resist, and the Ravenoserous thundered again, drool oozing from its jaws.

"Raaaaarrraarararar!" cried a voice.

It was the Narzat – again! – standing proudly and pounding his chest defiantly.

The Ravenoserous couldn't believe that he had forgotten about this roaring annoyance. Switching from the Chirper, it sprinted at the Narzat. But, yet again, a purple blur hit it square in the side as it ran. That darned Lizard was hurling things again! The Ravenoserous switched its course, running at the Looky Lizard.

"I'm actually quite low in fat as well, so I'd probably be quite a good dish if you've got a special event coming up, so I'm told. A *dandylion* on a diet once

27

told me that, which I think is a compliment, don't you?" squawked Chatty Chirper.

And so it continued. As soon as the Ravenoserous neared one of the friends, the others distracted him. If he wanted a chomp of a Chirper, a roar would offend him! If he wanted a Narzat Nibble, a pebble would sting him! If he wanted a lizard lunch, then a fussy bird would tempt him. The three friends – each determined to save the others – would do everything in their power to keep the beast busy.

Around and around the monster ran, charging this way and that, that way and this, until its feet ached and its roars turned into heavy panting. Soon the charging gave way to jogging, the jogging to trotting, the trotting to stumbling.

Night began to fall and the Ravenoserous – weary, exhausted and hungrier than ever – collapsed on to the floor and closed its eyes. Its roars were nothing compared to its snores, and the whole ground seemed to shake as it snoozed.

The three friends sprinted to each other, all smiles and relief, before embracing.

"But wait!" flapped the Chatty Chirper. "The sun's

almost gone – how are we ever going to see our way out of the Deep Dark Depths?"

The Looky Lizard gave a wry smile and straightened her back. With a little cough, she closed her eyes and bowed. The beautiful blue spirals on her back suddenly began to glow with the brightness of the sky on a summer's day.

Holding hands, the friends walked together out of the Deep Dark Depths with the light of the Looky Lizard guiding them. Although, if you looked very closely, you could see that their smiles were glowing too.

Chapter 5

The Three Friends

And so it was that the Narzat, the Looky Lizard and the Chatty Chirper became closer friends than there ever were. The trio were truly inseparable and every moment together was a smile, every day was a happy memory ringing with the sweet music of laughter.

That is not to say every day was perfect – no day ever truly is! The Chatty Chirper and the Looky Lizard could often bicker about the smallest nonsense, or find an argument hiding within the emptiest of spaces. If the Looky Lizard looked out on the golden sunrise and gestured:

That's the most beautiful sunrise ever!

The Chatty Chirper would tut, shake his head and reply:

"Oh no! It's probably in the top 20, but it's nowhere near the best! Last Monday had more warmth and there was one a couple of weeks ago that made the clouds look like coconuts – or was it Brazil nuts? It was certainly some kind of nut."

Looky would reply with:

You're some kind of nut.

And both would carry on bickering until the Narzat shushed them and tickled them together until they made up.

Please don't think that this was a sign that the bird and the lizard weren't actual friends. Only two creatures as close could truly annoy each other that much. They would always do kind things for one another, but in a sweet, quiet way – the Chatty Chirper would always pluck some of his softest feathers for the Looky Lizard to add to her blanket on cold nights, and she would leave little gifts of *mowberries* and *quango fruit* next to his nest for a breakfast surprise. Of course, if either of them ever thanked the other, they'd get terribly embarrassed and start arguing all over again.

The Three Friends would make all kinds of mischief and merriment within the Jumble Jungle Wood.

On cold days, they would venture to the frost swamps and throw great heaps of icy mud at each other. On warm days, they would climb to the top of a towering toomba and sunbathe on its triangular leaves. Sometimes, they would play hide and seek in the Peekaboo Fields, where the blades of grass are two metres tall. Other times, they would play jongo-ball with a herd of sly-hyenas (or *slyenas*), and spend half-time swapping jokes with them.

For treats, they would go digging for underground *chocotruffs*. These gooey lumps tasted of the sweetest chocolate, but unfortunately smelt and felt just like lumps of mud. The only way to tell if you had one was to take a bite. Many a dinner time was filled with the happy gnawing of the Narzat, or the startled squawk of the Chirper shouting: "Bleurgh! Mud... again!"

For dares, they would venture close to the raging rivers but none of them would go in. The Looky Lizard would always get closest, but surprisingly it was always the Narzat who lost. He had a deep, petrifying fear of water and he could not bring himself close enough without shaking. The Narzat fared far better on other dares, such as seeing who could tickle a *grumpus* or how high could someone climb a tree blindfolded.

On days where they fancied a bit of quiet, they would venture to a calm spot and find a *hug-a-slug* to cuddle. Back where you are, you probably would never want to hug a slug – and quite right you are! But to hug a hug-a-slug is another thing altogether. They are the size of a pillow but twice as squishy, and three times warmer. From head to tail, they are completely covered in the softest fluff, which ripples and shimmers like water. No two hug-a-slugs are the same colour, but all of them are as cuddly as the next. Whether of the brightest blue or the deepest purple, the only similarity in their appearance is their faces – a pair of bulging black eyes twinkle beneath the fluff, and a wide, dark grin spreads from cheek to cheek. Whenever you cuddle a hug-a-slug, one of three marvellous things might happen.

1. They release the softest squeal of delight before purring deeply.

2. Their antennae – resembling pom-poms on delicate stalks – will reach out to hug you back.

3. When they've had enough of you, they release a special slippy slime. If you're hugging them too hard, this often means that they shoot out of your arms and happily whizz off through the air.

The three friends would lie there for hours, cuddling the creatures, and smiling happily.

After a day of adventures, the three friends would often sneak off to a rocky outcrop and lie around the glowing flames of a *smallcano*, staring up at the twinkling lights of the stars above.  The smallcano (a tiny mountain, gently pulsing with a glowing red heat) would occasionally billow little clouds of smoke that floated high into the air above them. In some parts of the jungle, they say that if you dream hard enough, smallcanoes can paint your deepest hopes in smoke. In other parts of the jungle, they say that this is nonsense.

The three of them were lying there one evening when the Chirper squawked:

"Ooh! That cloud looked just like a nest full of eggs! Just like the one I grew up in!" He clapped his wings together. "Look! That one has even got freckles like my brother's egg! And that one's upside down like my sister Talky Tweeter – she was always doing handstands! I remember them all so well! And... and..."

The Chirper stopped and made a sound that neither of his friends had heard him make before. Silence. The Narzat sat up and saw that a small tear was rolling down his friend's beak.

"I remember them. All so well. But I miss them even more... I wonder if I will ever find them again?"

The Looky Lizard stood up, trotted over to the Chirper and wrapped her arms around him. As she did so, another puff of smoke erupted from the smallcano.

It looked like a circle of reptiles, just like her, holding hands. She took a step back and put a hand on her chest.

"Does that look like your family?" chirped the Chirper happily. The Lizard replied with a slow nod.

"What happened to them? I don't think you ever said! Ooh – we should invite them over for some chocotruffs or even a games evening!" babbled the bird, but he was interrupted by the Looky Lizard holding up a hand. Sorrowfully, she moved her body and did a gesture that she had done once before.

Ravenoserous.

Followed by:

They're all gone.

This time, the Chirper hugged her.

The Narzat walked over to both of his friends and placed a muddy hand on each of their shoulders. He growled softly as his brown eyes smiled with sympathy.

A puff of smallcano smoke caught his attention but he didn't quite understand it.

It showed two strange figures – one much larger

than the other – hugging. Amidst the wisps of smoke, he was sure he could see a smile and – deep within his memory – he heard the softest strains of a song. Although he didn't understand why, he found that he had tears in his eyes.

"I never realised," muttered the Chirper, "None of us have a family."

The Looky Lizard untucked herself from his wing and gave him a slight shove. Before he could squawk or bicker, her hands danced lightly in the night air.

Yes we do. We have us.

Chapter 6

The Jumble Jungle Café

Although the friends often ventured far and wide throughout the jungle, there were two places they often chose to avoid in particular. One was the Deep Dark Depths, and this was for obvious reasons, of course. Many, toothy, dangerous reasons. The second was somewhere far more pleasant, and far more surprising that it was avoided.

This place was the Watering Hole. Within the middle of the Jumble Jungle Wood, fringed by swaying palm trees, the Diamond Waterfall rushed and whooshed through the greenery. Plunging off a smooth pink cliff, it caught the light like a cascade of gems, and plummeted into a lake of the darkest black beneath.

As cool and inviting as the Dark Lake was, no animal dared to swim in it – it was deeper than the ocean; so deep that neither sunlight or moonlight could pierce its glassy surface. For those brave – or foolish enough to swim in it – there was the added danger of *dark weed*. Rumours whispered of slithering, slimy vines that stretched from the bottom of the lake, willing to pull any animal down to a watery prison. Some animals disagreed over whether this was true, but all of them agreed it was not worth testing to find it out.

Lining the edge of the Dark Lake, were several small ponds and pools – all of them of a far friendlier depth, and each one inviting in an entirely different way to the next. The animals of the jungle would flock to these in their masses, eager to bathe in the bubbling warm waters of a small soda stream, or cake themselves in the rich brown mud of the dirt pond. Nothing cooled a temper like the icy shallows of the frosty plunge pool, and nothing soothed an ache like the gentle warming of the eucalyptus puddle. The whole place seemed to bubble with the chatter and cheer of animals enjoying a good soak, as they lazed in the shade of the lush green leaves above and listened to the melodious splash of the waterfall.

Amidst all of this joy, lurked the Watering Hole's secret treasure. Carved into the cliff-face, a series of narrow steps wound and wended themselves up behind the waterfall. They led to a vast cavern full of large slabs of rock laid out into tables, and surrounded by the soft seating of bush pillows. Fireflies buzzed through the air, illuminating the cave with a warm orange glow, whilst the sound of the waterfall tinkled gently, echoing off the walls like a soft melody. Sitting in the cavern, you could look out through the rushing waterfall as if it were a giant frosted window.

This cave was the most popular place in the whole of the jungle and was known simply as *The Jumble Jungle Wood Café*.

At mealtimes, the entire place could be found awash with every possible animal. Slyenas chuckled away around tables, dandylions rubbed their green paws happily, and *tree cod* would slap the tables excitedly with their flippers. Animals were either excitedly waiting for a meal, or were joyfully reminiscing about the delicious treat that they had just enjoyed. Very few animals could be found eating – purely because when a meal arrived, it would be so delicious that it would be devoured in seconds.

Indeed! It is here where *hippo-roos* would eagerly bounce from one leg to the next as they devoured trays of grilled quango and square-pear ice-cream. *Chattermonkeys* would eagerly snaffle twice- roasted sugarnuts, whilst butterflies danced through the steam pouring off jungle-buns. Often, a group of *retractable giraffes* could be found drinking soothing fruit soup through long pine-straws. Other times, a group of *mockodiles* lay around an empty cauldron of vegan forest-chilli, chuckling as they patted their bulging bellies.

I would love to say that every animal in the Jumble Jungle Wood Café was overjoyed, or happy or even

just pleased. But that would not be true. In fact, nearly all of the animals sat grinning at the fullness of their belly and smiling at the dance of their tastebuds. All of the animals, apart from one… Pertinax, the Gorilla Chef.

Pertinax stood many metres tall, his broad shoulders rippling with muscle, and his broad belly rippling with dinner. His dark fur was matted with grease and stains of all manner of food, and he had wrapped a great dirty apron around his middle. Balanced on his head was a white chef's hat – it stood pristine and clean, and not so much as a speck of dirt had ever touched it. Pertinax would stomp and romp around the café, grumpily snatching plates and slamming down dishes. In a furry blur, he would swing from table to table, before jumping down next to a bubbling cauldron atop of a smallcano at the back of the cave. Here, he would bang and clatter, chop and crack, stir and whir, as he cooked up whatever the animals desired. His mighty fingers would nimbly move, crushing a walnut in his palm one second or delicately peeling a *mini-mini-mango* the next.

No one ever complained about the food – not just because it was so delicious, but because rumour had it that Pertinax had once thrown an entire table through the waterfall in annoyance when someone had mentioned that their trifle was a little salty. No one ever complimented him about the food either. If someone stopped to say to Pertinax that the meal was delicious, he would loom over them and growl: "What do you mean?" If someone told him it was the finest chilli they had ever had, he would crack his knuckles and grumble: "What's wrong with my other chillis?" Once, a particularly nervous flea had smiled at Pertinax, who bluntly roared at it for wasting his time. Very soon, the animals learnt that Pertinax did not like to stop and chat when he could be cooking. They would chatter, nervously make their order when he came rampaging past, chatter some more, silently sit as he slammed their order down in front of them, then happily continue their meal once he had moved on to his next table of terrified customers.

In spite of his fierce temper, the Jumble Jungle Wood Café was rarely less than full – which perhaps goes to show just how delicious Pertinax's food was.

It may surprise you that the Narzat, with his love of all things yummy and a taste for all things yucky, had avoided such a place. But, if you remember, he had a fear of water. Although you may say fear was not a strong enough word. He had an absolute terror of water, and he dared not venture any closer to it than he had to. The Narzat had once glanced the Watering Hole from afar, spotted the raging waterfall and the Dark Lake, and vowed to never go there ever. Never ever. Never ever ever ever.

You have to be careful when you say *never*. Sometimes things happen, wonderful unpredictable things that you could not have possibly seen coming. And these things have a wonderful way of undoing all of the "*never*" promises that you have ever made.

In the case of the Narzat, the thing that undid his promise was a rather hungry Chatty Chirper.

Chapter 7

Diving In

The Narzat was cheerfully trampling through the forest with the Chatty Chirper and the Looky Lizard. All three friends had spent a merry morning climbing to the tops of the tallest towering toombas and grabbing huge scoops of cloud-blossom to throw at each other. As they wandered through the forest, the Chatty Chirper raised a wing, and his curved beak began to twitch.

"I say! Can you smell that? You must smell that. You have to smell that!" he burbled, hopping from one foot to the other.

The only thing I can smell is you, beaky! signed the Looky Lizard, shooting a smirk at the Narzat. Her smirk changed, and she slithered forward. Her nostrils flared and her eyes widened.

Woah. Actually, I can smell something! she danced.

A loud growl interrupted them. The Narzat jumped back, fists in the air and eyes narrowed. He roared something that sounded like: "raveonserous!!"

"Um...no, sorry. It's not a ravenoserous..." muttered the Chatty Chirper, bashfully scratching a circle in the ground with his foot. "That might be my belly growling. What do you expect? Clambering up trees all day is bound to work up an appetitie!"

The Looky Lizard raised an amused eyebrow, and the bird stuck an annoyed tongue out at her. The Narzat leaned forward, his small nose twitching, and caught the scent too. Raising one arm, he bellowed and charged off into the forest.

Looky and Chatty shrugged at each other in a way that agreed they'd finish their argument later and charged after him. After many, many minutes of wending this way, bending that way and a fair old amount of hop, skip and jumping, the three friends crashed through the leafy undergrowth and paused.

They were stood on top of a small hill, overlooking the Watering Hole. Needless to say, taking in the mere sight of the deep lagoon and the crystal waterfall, two of the friends were delighted but one was absolutely terrified.

The Narzat froze to the spot, his mouth and eyes both hanging so wide open that the pinkness of his tongue clashed with the whiteness of his petrified stare. He gargled and tried to move his foot, but found that it had frozen to the ground. Shivers stampeded up and down his spine, and his stomach twisted painfully. The Chatty Chirper wrapped a wing around him and tried to usher him forward, backwards or sideways but he would not budge.

There's a wonderful saying in the Jumble Jungle Wood. Always look out for hippo-roos. These huge creatures (also known as *kangapotamuses*) are as huge as they are energetic, and they happily bounce on their bulbous bellies around the jungle. Many a poor animal has been nudged, knocked or even trampled by an oblivious hippo-roo.

And this is what happened to the Narzat.

A bounding hippo-roo sailed through the air, its warty belly slapping the back of the Narzat as it bounded down towards the Watering Hole. It grunted an apology as it splatted down into a mud pool, but it was too late.

The Narzat had been knocked, rolling down the hill – a blur of hands and feet. He managed to stop himself a breath away from the edge of the deep pool, and screamed. Scrabbling backwards on his hands and feet, he felt a splash of water touch his hand from a diving hippo-roo. He leapt to his feet and stumbled, almost falling into one of the many ponds.

Animals of all shapes and sizes – animals who had all been bathing in the many ponds of the Watering Hole – started to approach him with concern. But they were all soaking wet and the Narzat was convinced that they would throw him into the water. He flailed his arms and ran, hurtling towards the pink cliffs in front of him. Stairs! He had found stairs! His heart thundered as he charged up them and burst into a large cave… The Jumble Jungle Wood Café.

"Oi! What are you doin' runnin' in here!" bellowed a voice. Pertinax the Gorilla slammed down a wok so hard that it flattened into a frying pan and paced towards the Narzat.

"You, lad! What you doin' runnin' in my café! No one runs in my café!"

The Narzat stared, his eyes wide with terror, and pointed in the direction of the water. Was this gorilla going to make him leave? Was he going to make him go back out there?

"What you doin' pointin'?! Answer me!" roared Pertinax, bits of yesterday's banana flying out of his mouth.

You've heard of the Jungle saying: "Always watch out for hippo-roos" but there's an even sillier saying in the world. You may have heard some ill-advised adults say it back home. Some people say, "Fight fire with fire." To be honest, this is a stupid idea. If you want less fire, the last thing you want to add is more fire. Unfortunately, with the flaming fear burning oh so horribly hot inside the Narzat, the scorching shouting of Pertinax was not helping one little bit. In fact, it made matters worse.

The Narzat stumbled backwards, slipped on a bit of a banana (which would have been funny, had he not been so upset) and flew into the air, before landing on his back.

In the sudden kerfuffle, he felt something brush past his chin. Grasping at his neck, he realised. His shiny. His precious, important shiny. His one and only treasure. Terrified, he turned round and saw it sailing out of the window, through the crystal waterfall and... towards the deep, deep depths of the Dark Lake outside. He screamed, ran to the window, and placed his hands round his head. Sometimes, people are so sad that even their tears won't leave them. This is what was happening to the Narzat, and he stood, shaking and staring at the water that had stolen his most precious possession.

"Wh... what's happened!?" came a familiar squawk. The Chatty Chirper had arrived, breathless, having sprinted after his friend. He and the Looky Lizard had been knocked apart by the bouncing hippo-roo and had split up to search for the Narzat.

"What's happened?" repeated the Chirper. The Narzat would not reply. He could not reply.

"He had a shiny," rumbled Pertinax, leaning forward on his mighty hands. Pounding his knuckles into the floor, he strolled forward. "It looked important. And now it's in there."

He gestured a bandaged finger at the Dark Lake. That deep, dark lake where the sunlight barely scratched the surface. That deep, dark lake where no animals dared swim. The Chatty Chirper looked at his sobbing friend, and knew what he had to do. The problem was he really did not want to do it.

"Um... I'm sure we could find him another shiny? I saw a lovely one hanging up at jungle flea market or it might have been a swamp, I'm not sure but I remember thinking – wow! That could make a bracelet or phwerg!"

The Chirper did not actually say "phwerg!" It's just that Pertinax had clamped a pair of fingers round his beak in a way that said "I won't hurt you but I could."

He raised a chunky finger and pointed out of the window.

There was a small gap of lake between the cliff face and the base of the waterfall, where the dark water foamed white. The rocks had been polished smooth, and a small ledge jutted out into the water. Precariously lying on the edge of the rock, the Narzat's treasure dangled. And it appeared to be slipping.

Pertinax scratched his head – he appeared to be blushing in embarrassment.

"I wish I could climb down to get it, but what if I fell in… You see I can't swim," he grumbled. "Can you?"

The Chirper nodded, his beak still gripped firmly.

"I won't lie. It's going to be hard. Real hard," continued the mighty gorilla, "But nothin' worth doin' is ever easy."

He released the bird, who gasped for breath. The Chatty Chirper looked from the sobbing Narzat, to the nodding gorilla, and straightened his back. He gulped and took a step back.

The Looky Lizard bounded into the cave, saw one

friend muddily shaking, and one preparing to run at a window.

What are you doing?! she signed frantically.

The Chatty Chirper gave the shortest answer he had ever given in his life.

"Something difficult."

He ran, leapt and spread his wings. I would love to say he flew elegantly towards the ledge below, but the kindest thing I can say is that he slowly fell with style.

Flapping wildly, he landed on the rock. The stone surface had been polished smooth by spray from the waterfall, and the Chirper felt his feet racing against each other. He gripped the cliff face to steady himself.

The Narzat had heard the squawk of the Chirper's fall, and had edged himself to the window. Seeing his friend dive for the necklace did not make him feel better though – oh no. One of his best friends was now facing up to something incredibly dangerous, and there was nothing he could do about it.

The Chirper slowly shuffled across the stone. The shiny was more visible now. A length of the chain hung off the edge of the rock, and the whole locket seemed to be sliding gradually over the slippery surface. Gulping, the Chatty Chirper shuffled forward. He reached, stretching out his wing slowly. The chain of the shiny was a feather's width away.

The Chirper reached some more, and moved his talon carefully. The tip of his wing closed around the edge of the chain and… he slipped.

His feet started racing again – and the Chirper found his body whirling.

There was a splash and he sank beneath the surface. Icy cold water wrapped around him, the chill piercing his very bones. The darkness of it slipped over his eyes and the whole pool seemed to squeeze the breath out of him. Kicking his legs, he managed to poke his head above the water.

"I've got the shiny!" he squawked, breathless and proud. He bowed his head and began to swim.

But the Diamond Waterfall was having none of it. The churning water began to suck the Chirper back towards it, and the foaming spray blurred his sight. All he could see was white.

"Umm… help… I think I'm stuck!" he spluttered, kicking more and more. But the more he paddled, the more he realised… he wasn't going anywhere. The water was pulling him back.

Suddenly, something shone through the blur of the foam. A small blue light pulsed and flashed before him. It could only be the Looky Lizard.

The Chirper pushed some more, kicking ferociously. He could see his friend more clearly now. She had climbed down after him, and was leaning over the edge. The bird reached out towards her, but the tips of his wing were just out of reach of her hands.

The Looky Lizard narrowed her eyes, before glowing and waving one word desperately at him.

Shiny.

The Chirper realised it was clenched in one wing, and he swung the chain up towards his reptile friend. She caught it with one hand and heaved.

Far above, watching from the wide window of the Jumble Jungle Wood Café, a herd of different beasts – dandylions, hippo-roo, chattermonkeys, hug-a-slugs, and more – had gathered in stunned silence. At their centre, the Narzat watched – his terror now turning into horror as his two best friends had been immersed in his worst fear. He had never felt so utterly alone. Suddenly, something warm draped over his shoulders, like a blanket. Something warmer rested on his head. Pertinax, the huge, shambling gorilla, was cuddling him.

"It'll be OK lad. It'll be OK," he whispered.

As the Chirper drifted in the water, short of breath, the wetness stinging his eyes, he kicked his legs desperately. The Looky Lizard dug her feet into the rock and heaved the chain with both hands. The Chirper was not being pulled back towards the waterfall any more, but neither was he going forward. And they were both running out of energy.

"Something's touching my leg! Something's touching my leg!" shrieked the Chirper. "It must be dark weed or – oh, it's my other leg!"

The Lizard's glowing blue light pulsed. As it did so, it illuminated the locket hanging in the middle of the chain. Both friends could read the words inscribed in its centre.

When the night is long and dark,
We fear the sun shan't rise.
But oh – my love – soon it does,
And what beauty fills our eyes!

The second they finished the last line, their eyes locked. They nodded at each other. With one last heave from the Looky Lizard, and a huge kick from the Chirper, the bird broke free from the grip of the waterfall. With a splash, and a crash, he burst from the surface and tumbled upwards on to the rocky ledge. Gasping for breath, they lay there for a second before looking up the cliff-face.

"I've – we've got your shiny!" called the Chirper. Even though the Diamond Waterfall still continued to splash and foam, he could hear the rapid applause of the animals in the Café. And no applause was louder than that of the Narzat.

After climbing their way back up a make-shift ladder (made with the help of a *triple-trunked mammoth* and a couple of friendly pythons), the Chatty Chirper and the Looky Lizard staggered over to the Narzat. They presented him with the shiny, and he cradled it to his heart before embracing them both. He realised that as much as he treasured his only possession, there were two more things that were far more precious to him.

***

Hours later, the three friends were sat happily around the table with full bellies and full smiles. Pertinax had prepared a truly delicious feast for them. Steaming fruit soup, followed by mudburgers in jungle buns and sweet turnip fries, all topped off with the finest chocotruff ice cream. When they explained they could not pay, the Gorilla Chef growled at them. Everyone paid for their food in the Jumble Jungle Wood Café and the price was always the same. You had to do something kind.

Pertinax explained to them that they had already paid for many, many meals, before shuffling away. The Narzat wasn't sure, but he thought that he might have even seen the chef smile. As he watched the lumbering beast place beautiful bowls and perfect plates of delicious dinners in front of more grinning animals, he realised that there was more to Pertinax than he had thought.

The Looky Lizard turned to the Chatty Chirper.

Chirper? I've got a question, she gestured.

"Fire away!" grinned the Chirper.

You didn't seem scared, earlier. I mean… when I found you.

"Nope!"

But… I mean this nicely… You're a wuss!

The Chirper laughed.

58

"I know I am!" he squawked.

But, I mean, weren't you scared? Scared that you were lost?

"Oh! I was never lost!" chuckled the Chirper. "I always knew that you would find me."

If I could finish the story here, you would all agree that this is a wonderful tale of friendship, happiness and heroism. But, I'm afraid that the story does not finish here. You cannot always have light without the dark and darkness was coming. Darkness was coming to the Jumble Jungle Wood.

Chapter 8

Darkness in the Jungle

The day had started like any other. After a breakfast of rolled honey-leaves and roasted square-pear, the Narzat climbed trees whilst his two friends argued. They continued the morning's fun with a game of Snakes and Ladders: the Narzat had a whale of a time climbing ladders fashioned out of vines so he could surf down a slimy python. In case you're worrying, the python actually found this quite enjoyable and thanked the Narzat for the back massage.

BANG!

A sound like a thunderstorm happening all at once echoed through the jungle. The Chatty Chirper squawked and leapt into the arms of the Looky Lizard, and the Narzat paused mid-surf. The bang was louder than anything they had heard before – and they had been roared at by the Ravenoserous! – yet it sounded so far away.

The day seemed to continue as normal. After a quick mud-wrestle in a particularly disgusting bog, the trio sat down for lunch at the Jumble Jungle Wood Café.

BANG!

The sound seemed to shake the air. In the kitchen, Pertinax dropped a plate and started shouting. Looking out of the window, the Narzat saw a pale

flamingo – completely drained of its usual pinkness – soaring rapidly through the air. It screamed as it flew, casting quick looks over its shoulder.

In the afternoon, the friends decided to find a group of hug-a-slugs to settle their nerves and maybe find a *giant lily-apad* to curl up on for a nap. As the Narzat had grown tired with walking for the day, he decided that they should have a race along the tree tops to get there.

And so it was that they bounded through the jungle canopy. The Looky Lizard somersaulted and glided from twig to twig, barely disturbing a single leaf in her acrobatics. The Narzat joyfully snatched at vines and branches as he swung his body through the trees, stopping to scream happily as he did so. Meanwhile, the Chatty Chirper lagged behind, clumsily bouncing off one trunk and on to the next whilst branches smacked him in the beak.

BANG!

The deathly noise boomed. Next to the Chatty Chirper, a bough of leaves erupted into a shredded green cloud as a branch seemed to be sliced off the tree by some invisible force. The poor bird whimpered and darted back amongst the canopy, wrapping a vine around himself.

The Narzat – who was only a few metres in front – froze.

"Missed! Curse that damned pigeon!" growled a voice. Not a happy voice, not even an annoyed voice but a truly angry voice. It bubbled with fury, like a boiling pot about to lose its lid.

"I'm sure it's probably dead from shock... or embarrassment at your appalling aim," replied another voice. Although this voice was not as angry as the first, it was no less unpleasant. It dripped with disdain as though each syllable detested having to be spoken.

In the treetops, the Looky Lizard scampered back to sit on the Narzat's shoulder, as he lowered his head silently and looked down.

At first, he saw something utterly bizarre. It looked like an immense pile of bags and sacks and boxes shuffling along on two legs. We would have called this pile luggage (actually, we would have called this pile *a lot* of luggage). But behind this pile was something that caught the Narzat's attention even further.

I told you earlier that the Narzat had only ever encountered three things that he did not want to be friends with straight away. One was the Ravenoserous. The other two, the owners of the two voices, were stood directly beneath him, and they were far, far worse. They were also two creatures that the Narzat had never seen before: humans.

The first person, seen from above could be mistaken for a giant toad. He was as wide as he was tall, his legs squarely planted on the ground and he wore a huge hat. Below the hat, his eyes

darted about hungrily as if looking for something to eat, the whole jungle perhaps. His face was shiny and pink and his many chins quivered with anger. Were it not for the wisps of grey hair surrounding the back of his head, or the fantastically bushy moustache that crawled from ear to ear via his enormous nose, or the large monocle resting over one of his beady eyes, you could very easily mistake his head for a giant boil. Perhaps to fool others, or perhaps even to fool himself, he had tried to look the part of an explorer and had clad himself in expensive exploration clothes – from perfectly creased shorts, a rounded jungle hat and a crimson scarf, he had clearly felt that he had dressed for the Jumble Jungle Wood – but it just looked fake, like a man who had rented an outfit and wasn't quite sure what to do in it.

This man was none other than Lord Snide, and he could easily have won the prize for the greediest, most despicable human that ever there was... were it not for his wife.

Lady Snide was an icicle in human form, only twice as cold and three times as sharp. The only things that were of any interest to her in the world were Lady

Snide, and things that might benefit Lady Snide. If something did not fall into one of those categories, it was disregarded immediately.

Famously on their travels, the Snides encountered a pair of starving polar bears. Lady Snide saved the larger of the two, had it transported back to their estate (at great cost, might I add) and nurtured it back to health until it was as wide as her husband. Strangely enough, the world's press saw every second of this – the photographs of tears cascading down Lady Snide's face; artists' portraits of her giving the bear daily baths until its fur was as white as snow; the sound recordings of her voice trembling as she reported on the bear doing oh so wonderfully; her public messages about how she wished she had the time and strength to save more poor bears. The country was awash with whispers about Fair Lady Snide – *Oh! Isn't she kind?* And

She does so much for others! And even the frightful *I wish I were more like her!* These whispers would have been well-deserved, were it not for the fact that if you went into Lady Snide's study, you would find a large, pristine polar bear rug stretching from corner to corner, as white as snow and nicely stretched by re-feeding.

Oh yes – Lady Snide made sure that she was seen doing "good deeds" and kept her real motives hidden. She donated money to orphanages in public events, but kept her new band of child servants at Snide Manor under wraps. She was a champion for local zoos, but no one noticed the new assortment of fur coats that Lady Snide suddenly seemed to be procuring. When she catered – free of charge – for her friends before an awards ceremony, no one noticed when they all vanished with food-poisoning and she was left to scoop up every trophy.

Never had the outward actions and appearance of someone so greatly differed from what lay within. On the outside, she had a fantastic smile that stretched from ear to ear. Those very ears sparkled with the finest diamonds – a sparkle that matched the bright green of her eyes. Her platinum hair had been lacquered to perfection and cascaded in coils around her smooth, unblemished face. Slender fingers dripped with bracelets and jewels. Whereas Lord Snide had dressed in a manner suited to the jungle but not to him, Lady Snide's clothing suited her not the jungle. A scarlet red suit, matching the scarlet red of her lips, flowed down the narrow contours of her body, whilst her shiny, black high heels caused her to tower even further above her husband.

To many people, she was strikingly beautiful. However, the Narzat shuddered at the sharpness of that smile and the cruel searching glances of those eyes – it reminded him too much of a crocodile waiting for its prey. The Looky Lizard noticed the redness of her nails and the redness of her suit – it reminded her of the most poisonous berries of the Deep Dark Depths. The Chatty Chirper, however, stared at the gold of her hair and nodded with approval.

The Snides, as you have gathered, were beastly rich and richly beastly. This meant that they were often surrounded by copious amounts of servants, who they enjoyed taunting berating and bullying. It seemed good sport to Lord Snide to make a maid cry most mornings, and Lady Snide would delight in causing butlers to tremble in angst over her evening tea.

How did the Snides manage to keep people to stick around for such abuse? The answer was simple... money. The Snides paid all of their servants well – although they were soon to discover that they did not pay quite enough.

On their journey to the Jumble Jungle Wood, the Snides had begun with a hearty crowd of servants. Lord Snide had taken a chef, a sous-chef, a pastry chef, a pasta cook, a party caterer, a master baker and a chocolatier – and a sandwich maker. Lady Snide had insisted on taking two jewellers, a team of make-up artists and a group of photographers to capture her beauty. Of course, they needed eight burly butlers to carry their luggage, several maids to tidy up after them, a chauffeur to drive, a spare chauffeur for when the first one got tired, valets galore to help them dress, and – for a reason no one was quite sure of – an elderly gardener called Mr Widdershins trotted along too.

The journey started in a bearably awful fashion. Lady Snide spat at a butler for not carrying her mirror at the right angle, and Lord Snide tipped an entire bowl of spaghetti over the pasta cook when it was not to his liking. When they started sailing across the first of many oceans, things got trickier. Their insults grew so foul, their tempers so huge, that several butlers leapt overboard and started swimming back to land to escape having to deal with their hateful bosses.

When they crossed the Whispering Desert, Lady Snide slapped a maid and punched a valet because she was fed up with how hot the sun was. The maid and valet promptly realised that the heat of the desert was no match for the heat of Lady Snide's temper, and promptly resigned.

The further they went, the trickier the trek became. And the trickier the trek became, the fouler the Snides were – which of course, led to even more servants departing. The master baker snapped in the middle of the Ice Lakes and skated back, the chauffeurs found

themselves driven away in the mud swamps, and the pasta cook climbed into his biggest pot next to the Raging Rapids of the Rangutan River, and sailed himself and the rest of the catering staff away.

Not even Mr Widdershins, as good-natured as he was, could put up with Lord Snide's daily insults or Lady Snide's casual cruelty. It had been a particularly hefty day, and they were camped a good week's walk from the Three-Headed Mountain. Mr Widdershins had already been shouted at twice that morning – for not growing Lord Snide a breakfast tree, or picking a rose that smelt as distinctive as Lady Snide. When they complained that his name wasn't entertaining enough, he said the first rude word he had ever said in his life and stormed off.

As they stumbled along the floor of the Jumble Jungle Wood, far below the watchful eyes of the Narzat and his friends, the Snides continued to bicker.

"This would be easier if you hadn't brought so much stuff and nonsense!" moaned Lord Snide.

"Oh, stop moaning you old hog!" shrieked Lady Snide. "It would be easier if you hadn't gone and lost our last proper servant."

"Shut up, wench!" boomed Lord Snide in reply. "It's your hideous moaning that got rid of *him*!"

"Hideous moaning!? At least, it's better than your hideous face!"

"There you go again, you trout-faced vomit-sack!"

Lady Snide raised herself to her full height and her thin lips drew themselves tight, baring her snarling, white jaws. "At least I can count!" she trembled, raising one scarlet clawed finger and pointing it at the bundle of bags and boxes and sacks. "We've got one servant left!"

Lord Snide's beady eyes followed his wife's out-stretched finger to glance at the pair of legs sticking out from beneath their luggage.

"*Her!?*" he snorted. "She doesn't count... We don't even pay her!"

"She works for us... and that means she counts as a servant. I don't know what else to call her," sneered Lady Snide.

They would have continued arguing for an hour and a day if they weren't interrupted by a slight, polite cough. Their enraged eyes flitted from each other to the owner of that very cough.

"Um.. excuse me..." politely sighed the person resting beneath the bags and boxes and sacks.

Lord and Lady Snide's voices unified with a disgruntled:

"What?!"

Slowly lowering the luggage, a small figure stepped out to greet them. Smudges of coal covered her face, and strands of her auburn hair whirled out in a tired frizz. A stained apron hung loosely from her tattered black dress, and her maid's hat sat askew on top of her bowed head. She politely smiled and said, "You could call me... Polly. It is my name, after all."

From where the Narzat and his friends sat, they could not quite see Polly. They leaned and jostled in the leaves to get a closer look at her, but found the mountain of the Snides' luggage blocked their view. Even so, they all heard her voice clearly. It had a gentle warmth to it, and reminded the Narzat of hugs and happiness. Had they been but a few metres to the left, or a few metres lower, they would have been struck by Polly's smile.

Polly's smile was

of wide renown amongst all the servants (that was before they had all left). They all had noticed how it always seemed ready to appear – when the insults of the Snides got to their worst, it would be there. When someone needed reassuring, it would be there. It truly was a wonderful smile – full of warmth and friendship – and it lit up her face like light on the ocean. Of course, because we are going to get to know Polly a bit better, we can take a closer look at the smile and see that there is something missing. No matter how happy it is, the smile never quite reaches her eyes. They were two pools of blue that had somehow lost their brightness, as though a sadness lurked there and would never leave.

Lord Snide had no time for happy smiles or sad eyes. He had turned purple at the interruption and his mouth swung open like a cannon preparing to launch an insult. Unfortunately for him, Lady Snide was far swifter in an argument. And far crueller.

"How long have we known you, dear?" she soothed in a voice as smooth as a hedgehog.

"Um… a long time…"

"How long?" continued Lady Snide, as sweetly as she could manage.

"Very long, Lady Snide. About 20 years, truth be told," Polly continued.

"And, during that time, have we ever shown the slightest interest in your name?"

"Ummm… no ma'am," sighed Polly.

"So…" smoothed Lady Snide, before shoving Polly in the chest, "shut up and put up with what we call you. Now get back to carrying those bags—"

A sudden squawk interrupted Lady Snide, as a large bird plummeted down in front of her. The Chirper had desperately been leaning forward to get a better view of these strange creatures, and had misjudged his grip on a twig. Picking himself up off the floor, he eagerly dusted off his dark blue plumage, and smiled up at Lady Snide.

"I'm terribly sorry for interrupting – I was just trying to get a good look at your hair! It's beautiful!" the Chirper cawed, puffing out his chest. "And I love the red of your fur – is it fur or is it feathers? I myself am quite a fan of vibrant colours! Look at *my* feathers – every colour of the rainbow!"

Lord Snide stepped forward, his chest and chins swelling. From the treetops, the Narzat noticed something clutched proudly in his fleshy palm. It looked like a long, slender stick that had been polished to perfection and it was smoking gently at the top. Lord Snide pointed it at the Chatty Chirper.

"Shut up, bird," he sneered. "I don't know what's more impressive – the fact that you can talk or the fact that every word is so irritating."

The Chatty Chirper gulped. Him? Irritating? He glanced indignantly at Lady Snide, who stepped forward and placed a hand on her husband's rifle (for that is what it was, Lord Snide's prize hunting rifle – were it not for the numerous notches carved on the side for every animal it had taken, one might have assumed it was brand new).

"Wait. The bird can talk. This could be useful," she declared, in a voice that sounded like champagne glasses clinking. "Imagine what the universities would say when I introduce them to this parrot and tell them that I trained it to talk! They'll think it marvellous… and I can even take it to Broadway to perform! Imagine what they'll say about Lady Snide – creator of talent! Champion of the arts! Discoverer of – Oh, hang on. You – parrot – can you sing?"

A dam of indignation had been holding back the

Chirper's offence, but this was enough – his shock flooded out.

"I AM NOT A PARROT!" he squawked, "I am a Chirper and I have been able to talk since I was an egg, thank you very much!"

Lady Snide raised a thin question of an eyebrow.

"So you won't tell people that I trained you?"

"No, madam! I will not!" retorted the Chirper, placing his wings on his hips.

Lord Snide nudged his wife.

"His feathers would make a nice hat," he drawled. Lady Snide nodded and turned her back.

The Chirper looked confused as Lord Snide raised that smooth, smoking stick and pointed it at him.

There was a sharp click, and a bang as loud as a thunder storm filled the forest.

Chapter 9

The Camp of the Snides

"He's a beast! A maniac! An absolute stench of a dungheap! Aargh! Mind your cold hands!" the Chatty Chirper fumed, outrage pouring from his beak.

Night had fallen in the Jumble Jungle Wood, and he lay stretched over an oversized coconut as the Looky Lizard applied cooling mud to his singed posterior.

"How dare he aim that sticky-boomy-boom-stick at me? Me? I was just saying OW! WHAT ARE YOUR HANDS MADE OF – ICE?"

The Looky Lizard shrugged before selecting an extra cold bit of mud to slap on next.

"It's a good job that Lady was there... The brave one. If she hadn't – OH MY TALONS! DON'T SMACK IT, YOU STUPID LIZARD! Humph... sorry... Now I've lost my chain of thought!" squawked the Chirper.

The Looky Lizard leaned out from behind him, icy mud in one hand and a mischievous glint in her eyes.

You were going to say... If that woman – Polly – hadn't grabbed that gun off that huge beast, you'd be toast.

Polly had indeed moved with incredible speed, pushing Lord Snide's gun to one side and preventing the Chirper from meeting a sticky end. Whilst the Snides had been busy shouting at her, the Narzat had clambered down the tree, grabbed his frazzled friend, and snuck back into the jungle.

"Precisely! I

must thank her and – OW! MY BOTTY! IS THAT MUD OR SANDPAPER!"

The Looky Lizard, trying to hide a giggle, leaned round and signed one more thing to the Chirper.

Who else are you going to thank?

"Oh yes! Thank you, I guess, for looking after me…" he turned his head, "And thank you Narzat for pulling me away to safety! Narzat. Narzat?"

But the Narzat did not respond. As he had rescued his friend, he had caught a quick glance at the startled maid. Now, he stood staring at the blue moon hanging over the jungle… that blue was the same shade of Polly's eyes and try as he might, he could've sworn he'd seen those eyes before.

***

A chilly breeze stalked through the Snides' camp, causing their fire to shiver. Had they put their tents 30 metres to the left, they'd have found a herd of hug-a-slugs ready to give a warming cuddle; if they had sat down 30 metres to the right, they may have found themselves in the golden glow of a small field of smallcanoes.

But the Snides had a history of poor choices. They sat, apart, in their large armchairs growling at the small camp fire. The flickering light glistened in the darkness of Lady Snide's pupils.

"Hurry up!" she barked, barely turning her head. "I mean, how long does it take to find a log?"

Behind her, Polly grunted as she staggered up to the fireside – her arms awash with firewood.

"It takes a while," she sighed as she plopped the logs on the floor, "especially when you've got to work out which one is a log and which one is a *log insect*."

"Log insect? Don't be ridiculous!"

snapped Lady Snide. As if to disagree, one log heaved itself up on to several tiny legs, and scurried into the woods. Log insects are quite common in the Jumble Jungle Wood, you see, but quite uncommon elsewhere. This is for 2 reasons – they are very convincing at being logs, and they absolutely adore sleeping amongst firewood.

"She is ridiculous," drawled Lord Snide. He had been staring into the darkness, wallowing in the muddy misery of a sulk. Pouting, he turned his sour expression to Polly.

"You cost me quite the prize. Again," he snarled.

"I could have shot that creature straight off. Just imagine! A photo of me brandishing that fowl, and right now, I could be dining on a steaming drumstick whilst *she*,' he jerked a thumb at Lady Snide, "could be amusing the feathers into a new hat or somesuch nonsense."

Lady Snide winced at the word nonsense but decided not to waste any of her bile on her husband. She stood up slowly, brushed the sequins on her dress and loomed over Polly.

"I don't like any of this. You're forgetting yourself. You've stopped Lord Snide from blasting that parrot. You've started answering back. You seem precoccupied… Have you forgotten why we're here?"

Polly's eyes flashed in a very Polly way, but she gulped down her snappy response and simply said, "No."

"No, what?"

"No… my Lady."

"Then why are we here?" continued Lady Snide.

Polly's eyes flashed again.

"Because Lord Snide wants to hunt and gobble up the most beautiful exotic creatures known to man, and you want to parade around in their skins?" she growled through gritted teeth.

Lady Snide laughed – cruelly – before shoving Polly so hard she almost tumbled into the fire.

"You forget… Those are perks – yes, but the real reason is that we must find that precious treasure. We know it must be here – years of research says it *has* to be here. You mustn't forget that… After all – it's your fault that it ended up here," continued Lady Snide. Tears welled up in Polly's eyes at the last point.

Lady Snide lowered herself into the chair.

"You've also forgotten one other thing, Polly… you are a log."

"What do you mean?" puzzled Polly.

"She means," barked Lord Snide – who had a habit of finished off his wife's nastiness. "She means you are a worthless piece of nothing that we might as well have picked off the floor. And, if we wanted to, we could get rid of you just like that."

His fleshy hand tossed a log on to the flames, as his booming laughter danced with Lady Snide's cruel cackle in the cool night air.

Chapter 10

Shushberries

Polly had been asked to fetch water for the Snides. Well, perhaps *asked* isn't the right word. Polly had been screeched at, bellowed at, pressured, bullied and ordered, commanded and demanded to fetch water for the Snides.

Having worked for them since she was small, she knew that arguing with them was pointless. As she dragged a battered bronze bucket out of the camp, memories tumbled through her mind of all the times she'd been landed with horrible chores from the Snides, and whether this would be one of the worst. She remembered having to polish all of Lord Snide's stinking boots as a child, and her hands being stained

with polish for days. She shuddered at how she'd had to burn all of Lady Snide's unwanted coats as a teenager, and how she'd got in trouble for trying to give the used clothes to charity. Polly was punished with no food or drink for a week, with only the stench of burning fabric sustaining her. Things continued to get worse in her twenties. From polishing every brick at Snide Manor, to clipping acres of green lawn with nail scissors, she'd been given every menial, mean task possible. As the base of the bucket scraped the ground, Polly at least reminded herself that this was different. She'd put up with all of these labours for so long so she could finally reach the Jumble Jungle Wood… and she was finally here.

Polly was so preoccupied with this thought that she did not notice a pair of eyes following her, as a dark Narzat shadow raced through the trees.

***

Back at the camp, Lord Snide lay snoozing in his camp chair. His great belly heaved, straining the stitches of his shirt. A silver sliver of drool stretched from his lips as vast snores rumbled.

Lady Snide – with ear muffs, ear plugs and a

towel wrapped around her head – was more adept at blocking out the snoring and slept silently – her face smothered in the remains of beetles she'd crushed that morning.

Still, someone was moving in the camp.

The Looky Lizard.

She'd carefully snuck in as soon as Polly left, and was nimbly ducking and diving behind the various possessions of the Snides. Crouching behind a stand full of ornate hats, she peered over at the slumbering Lord. He seemed awfully like the Ravenoserous to her.

Clutching a large bundle in her hands, her footsteps padded over the sand as she ducked behind a small kitchenette of pots and pans. She almost dropped what she was holding when she spotted an obscenely tall and cunning reptile towering above her. Looky raised a fist and an eyebrow.

I'm small but deadly. Come on then.

The giant reptile did the same. It took a moment for Looky to realise that this was in fact her reflection. She'd seen her reflection once before when practising amusing faces in the Diamond Waterfalls, but she'd never encountered a mirror before (and, as you can imagine, Lady Snide's mirror was suitably ornate and oversized).

Looky pressed on, crawling up Lord Snide's leg and reaching his outstretched arm. Delicately, she revealed what she was cradling – five shining purple *shushberries* – and placed them in his hand.

You may be thinking that this was a rather kind thing to do. After all, shushberries are a notoriously delicious fruit – they swim with sweetness and their juice tastes like liquid sunshine. But the Looky Lizard was not concerned with kindness. Oh no… Justice is what mattered to her. You see, shushberries have one curious side-effect: they are so delectable that their juice clings to the tastebuds, making the tongue go numb and the voice lose its shape. It is rumoured that the only way to reverse their effects are to immerse your head in cold water. In fact, if you visit the Crystal Rivers of the Jumble Jungle Wood, where the shushberry bushes grow, you will find clusters of chattermonkeys eating the berries underwater so they can enjoy the fruit and not suffer the side-effects.

As soon as the Looky Lizard had nestled the shushberries in Lord Snide's palm, she scurried away, hid behind an impossibly large trunk and waited. Lord Snide did nothing but continue snoring. Placing an exasperated hand on her face, she ran up and gave him a sharp kick in the shins. He yelped and leapt up, glaring away.

"Who the what now?" he barked.

Glancing around and finding no one to be angry with, he sighed and sank back into his chair. It was then he spotted five small berries cradled in his hand.

Instantly, he threw them in his mouth. They were, without a doubt, the juiciest, fruitiest delicacy he had ever sampled.

Yet the more he chewed, the less his mouth moved. Indeed the berries seemed to ooze out around his teeth and pour down his throat.

Barely opening his mouth, Lord Snide looked up and cried: "Schnarg! Schmarf!"

He leapt from his chair, knocking over the mirror and waking Lady Snide.

"What is it, you great oaf?" snapped Lady Snide, her giant sunglasses reflecting the purple of her husband's face.

What Lord Snide wanted to yell was, "Can't you see? I can't speak you stupid woman!" but what he actually shouted was: "Pooky pooky poo poo!"

"Why are you prattling on, you oaf?" snarled Lady Snide.

"Gimble fimble, oogly boogly!"

"What do you mean? Who are you calling 'Gimble Fimble'!"

"Oog!"

"Oog?"

"Oogly!"

At this point, the Looky Lizard rolled out from her hiding

place, clutching her stomach in silent laughter. She was wracked with giggles and her blue stripes shone as she shook. In her silent commotion, she caught Lord Snide's angry gaze. And though not the most understanding man, Lord Snide certainly understood who she was laughing at.

"Gleeba schwiz! Woobly wee! Clamble fon gamble bodey barg!" he yelled, pointing at the Lizard and shoving his wife towards her. Lady Snide took one look at the Lizard, shrieked in rage, and drove a spiked heel down towards her. Looky was no stranger to people trying to look down and stamp on her, but she was also no push over. Gracefully, she dodged and jumped on to Lady Snide's foot, corkscrewing round her leg.

"Get it off me! Get it off me!" squealed the wretched woman, pawing at her dress as the Lizard whirled round towards her neck line.

Lord Snide grabbed his trusty rifle and aimed at the creature. Lady Snide slapped him round the chops.

"FOWS!"

"What are you doing pointing a gun at me? Bat it off!"

Lord Snide looked round and saw the dying embers of a log next to their wash bucket. He raced towards it.

"Google pep!" he oozed, raising a finger.

Looky bounced on to Lady Snide's chin and grabbed her flaring nostrils. She giggled as the enraged aristocrat whirled her arms, spinning in a circle. Suddenly, Lady Snide tripped, falling face first towards the dust in front of her husband.

Looky Lizard dived to one side, giggled some more, and raced off to the forest. Had she stayed a moment longer, she would have seen Lord Snide stumble over his wife's outstretched body and fall – landing head first into the wash bucket.

He leapt up, water spilling down his neck, with the bucket wedged on his head.

"This blasted bucket is stuck on my – wait! I can talk!"

"More's the pity…" sneered Lady Snide, standing up and dusting off.

"Shut up you nitwit," snapped Lord Snide, blindly whirling round and pointing at a tree. " Pull it off my head. Get that Polly to help!"

"She's not here," sneered Lady Snide. "She's off

getting us more water… and doing it slowly. She's useless."

"Useless," sulked Lord Snide in agreement, plonking

himself down in a chair. He missed and landed sorely on the floor.

Lady Snide moved to her husband and briefly considered placing a reassuring hand on his shoulder. Instead, she rapped on the bucket on his head.

"Where the devil is she?"

Chapter 11

Snakes and Gladders

Polly was making her way through the dense greenery. As the jungle pressed around her, she couldn't help but glance up at the rainbow of flowers above, or smile at the late morning chorus of hoots and whistles. So captivated was she, that she did not notice the shadow of the Narzat stalking in the treeline behind her. He nimbly darted and whirled through the vegetation, never taking his eyes off of Polly.

After many, many more minutes, the trees parted to reveal a grand clearing – to Polly, it looked like someone had stuck a beach in the middle of the Jumble Jungle Wood. Soft golden sand stretched across the floor, with a green path of grass cutting through its centre. At the end of this grassy trail lay a large green dome, completely made up of giant leaves curling over one another.

Polly took a step forwards onto the grassy path and, as if sensing her presence, the dome began to unravel and unfurl. The leaves slowly parted, and a large stem unravelled upwards – like a giant, towering neck – and at its head was the most dazzling flower Polly had ever seen. It was almost as large as her, and five pointed petals beamed from a dark, circular centre. The petals shimmered, flickering between blocks of bright colours. One second a petal would flash a bold yellow, before changing to a vibrant pink or a deep blue. The flower swayed neatly, seeming to stare at Polly, and lowered itself down. The petals flashed some more, bewitching a smile from her.

Mesmerised, Polly stepped forward.

The flower slid out a large, cupped leaf – about the size and depth of a bath tub – full to the brim with sparkling water. It tilted its flashing petals towards it, beckoning.

Polly gasped – what luck! She began to step forward... and tripped.

A rope had wrapped round her ankles. No – was it a vine? As she untangled her binding, her fingers were met with slimy scales. This was no vine... it was a tail.

Gasping – not screaming, nor screeching for she was not one for either of those – she clambered to her feet, kicking her legs. The tail slithered, revealing its owner – a long, skinny snake. Its khaki, cracked skin oozed with slime as a pair of yellow eyes stared from its wide, smirking face. Protruding from its lopsided grin was a solitary curved fang which glinted at a sharp point.

Polly stepped back and almost tripped again – another one of these snakes, long and impossibly bony, had slithered under her feet. Soon there were more snakes, slithering along the path, almost circling her, until they blocked the way to the flower. Leaning against each other, the snakes seemed to heave themselves upright until they were balancing on the tips of their tales, blocking Polly from continuing along the path.

Were you or I to meet a wall of scales, smirks and fangs, we'd probably turn and leave. Or run. Or scream. Or run screaming. But not Polly. Oh no… she had a job to do.

"Move it! You… you…snakes!" she cried, swinging the bucket into their stomachs.

The snakes fell to the floor, smirks replaced by affronted frowns. Polly's words had hurt them far more than her bucket and they slunk away. Polly grinned at the ease of her success and returned to the flower.

It had leaned further forward, gesturing gently to the pool of water. The stem lowered down, slithering along the ground as if trying to encircle Polly. Other leaves reached out, seeking to embrace her and gesture for her to come closer. The petals flashed and flushed quicker and quicker still – their beauty a kaleidoscope telling Polly… just one more step… just one more step…

"Ggggraaarg!" bellowed a voice behind her. The Narzat had landed on the grassy path and was sprinting towards her.

But Polly had already taken that step.

With a flash, two giant leaves swept forward and knocked Polly into the pool of water. As she reached up to gasp for air, the leaves closed around her forcing her under. The breath left her lungs as she grappled and scraped at the leafy walls.

The Narzat ran up to the leaves, pounding and scratching at the sides as he heard Polly's frantic thrashing around. He could make out a dark silhouette through the green – and she was churning in pain.

The flower changed colour to a deep scarlet, the petals closing together to a sharp point. It lowered its viny neck, launching at the Narzat's face and hissed.

He sprang back in time as the petals clamped together, their razor-sharp edges slicing through the air.

The plant launched at him again, spearing the ground and tearing the grass away. The Narzat sprang to the side as another leaf knocked him to the floor.

Wrestling in the dark greenness of the leaves, Polly felt her chest tightening. The cold water made her shimmer and shake. She kicked at the leaves some more, pawing at them with all of her might. They parted briefly and she pulled her face to gasp for air. The plant's water had stung her eyes and blurred her vision, but she was fairly sure she could see the oddest creature – a small muddy monster – battling a giant flower.

The Narzat lay on his back as the flower pounded at him again. He rolled to the side, just in time as it speared the ground with a sharp hiss, its raised petals widened and trembled with rage. The Narzat took two paces backwards and his back was now to Polly's leafy prison. Through the crack of sunlight, Polly could see what he was planning.

The flower launched itself at the Narzat one last time. He dove to the side as it burrowed into the pod of water. As the flower shattered and tore through its own leaves, Polly grabbed the neck of the stem and held it in the water with all her might. The flower shook and hissed, as the cold water closed round it. With a sudden jerk upwards, it freed itself from its own trap, pulling Polly free too.

She tumbled through the air, burrowing into the Narzat, causing them to fall backward. The flower snapped out at them, but they lay just out of reach. They collapsed, panting on the sand, a good few feet away from its biting petals. With a low hiss, the stem recoiled and the flower seemed to shrink back into itself, closing its leaves around itself until nothing was visible but a smooth green dome.

Polly turned to face her saviour, her eyes still blurry from the water. Taking in the outline of his

grimy face and the leaves in his hair, all she could do was whisper.

"Thank you. I mean… thank you," she croaked. Yet she had spoken too soon.

The ground seemed to be sinking beneath them. Polly tried to stand but she couldn't. The more she pulled her body up, the more the sand pulled her downwards. Glancing round, she heard the Narzat as he tried to lift his feet clear. He too was sinking.

"Don't move!" squawked a friendly voice. "You're in very quick sand. It's like quick sand but… um… quicker!"

Perched in front of Polly, on the grass path, was the bird from the day before, the creature she'd saved. He beamed through his banana beak.

"Oh – hello! Nice to have time to introduce myself properly this time! I felt horrendously rude for not doing it before. I'm the Chatty Chirper! I enjoy evening strolls, lemon drizzle cake and—"

"Grrrraaar!" roared the Narzat .

The Chirper slapped one wing to his forehead, and gestured to his sinking friend.

"My apologies. And you've already met my friend the Narzat!"

The Narzat roared again, this time sounding at once like a plea for help and an annoyed growl. The sand was round his waist.

"Well! Don't take that tone with me – look at the mess you've gotten yourself into. It's a good job I followed you! Anyway, I was talking to this lady. Sorry – you are…?"

"Sinking! Help please!" shouted Polly.

"Oh yes! Sorry! Always end up chatting when I shouldn't! Two ticks!" chuckled the Chirper. He vanished into the undergrowth, as Polly found herself dropping further.

"Glarg!" growled the Narzat – the sand was up to his armpits now.

"Here we are! I've brought help!" declared the bird. He was on the grassy path… surrounded by the single-toothed smirking snakes from before.

"No! Not them!" shrieked Polly.

The snakes, looking affronted again, turned around and started to slide back.

"Wait! Stop! She didn't mean it!" cawed the Chatty Chirper before turning to Polly. Lifting a wing, he leaned forward and whispered harshly. "They said you'd already offended them once when they were trying to help!"

"Help?"

"Yes! They tried to stop you being eaten up by that *snap-snap dragon flower*! And you were so rude to them!"

"But they were hissing – and showing their fangs… and – and – smirking!"

Polly, now with her arms and head above the sand, could not help but argue.

"Of course they were! These are *gladders*! They are glad to help anyone… but due to their… uh, unfortunate appearance they can be very easily offended. As for the smirk, have you ever tried grinning nicely with only one giant fang?"

Polly – with difficulty – shook her head.

"Now – ask for their help… and do it politely."

As her chin sunk further, Polly blurted out her apology.

"I'm so sorry – you were being kind and I was so rude… But please, *please* help us!"

The snakes stopped slithering away but did not turn round. Polly could only see the Narzat's hands poking above the surface.

"At least save the other creature – the Narzat! He's done nothing wrong but be brave and kind and…"

The sand closed around her.

Darkness.

She felt a scaly tail wrap around her wrist and another tail wrap around the other. Slowly, she felt herself being pulled up and away, the sand falling away from her until she lay, panting on the grassy path, the sun above her and smirking gladders surrounding her… and that strange creature – the Narzat – lying panting for breath beside her. The Chirper was standing on his chest, fussily brushing sand off himself. Flicking grit from her face, she sat up.

"Thank you! Thank you! You're too kind – I

shouldn't have judged you!" she panted to a gladder, who she swore she saw blush.

"And it's Polly," she smiled, turning to the Chirper. "My name's Polly."

Chapter 12

Tea Time with Polly

Polly followed the Narzat as he gambolled and pranced through the trees ahead of her. He would stop on occasion and shoot her glances through the green shade, and grunt at her whenever he felt she was about to trip. Polly's sight was still returning after struggling in the pool of the snap-snap dragon (the plant's water was designed to dull the senses) and she could increasingly make out the figure of this curious creature. He was a little taller than half her height, and his hands – though matted with mud and leaves – still seemed almost humanoid. What was he? Some kind of monkey? Polly had heard tell of "the missing link" before, but she could not remember what this was exactly. This was not because of her memory, but because the Chirper would not stop chattering in hear ear as he lolloped alongside her.

"Humans? I think I've seen your kind before! I must say that those two are particularly repulsive though – the blob and the sharp one. But you're alright. Not alright – fantastic! I never thanked you for saving me from that boomy stick thingy. Why does he have that? Is it for parties?" he babbled at her as she ducked under branches, and jumped over roots.

The Narzat would pause and wait for them, the wideness of his grin shining in the shade, before he scurried on ahead.

Eventually, he came to a stop. There seemed to be nothing remarkable about this patch of the jungle compared to anywhere else, but he stood and grinned.

"We're here!" beamed the Chatty Chirper.

"Where?" replied Polly.

"Here!"

"Where's here?"

The Chatty Chirper tilted his head to one side. Maybe humans were a bit simple. He slowly replied, "Well… here is the place you get to when you're not there."

Polly was too polite to point out when someone was being so ridiculous that they mistook a reasonable question for stupidity, so she simply smiled. The Narzat beckoned her closer – and then shot up a tree (a towering toomba, to be precise). Athletically swinging from branch to branch, he waved at Polly to follow.

She climbed after him for what seemed like an age, occasionally slipping on the soft bark, but never letting that stop her. The Chirper perched on her shoulder offering encouragement, or rather, what he thought was encouragement.

"There you go! Not bad for a first climb – I'm assuming you've never climbed before! You don't look like the type who does much climbing or movement. Oops! Almost hit me there!" he grinned.

Suddenly, Polly burst through the leaves above and what beauty met her eyes.

A sea of incredible green stretched out before her, glistening in the sun. Far in the distance, the Three-Headed Mountain loomed – piercing the blanket of blue above them. To her left, she could see the changing colours of the trees of the Jumble Jungle Wood, and far to her right she could spy small

plumes of smoke (from the smallcano fields). The sky was cloudless – well, almost, as one angry grey cloud lurked over the Deep Dark Depths in the far distance. Vibrant birds burst from the tree line and sailed peacefully in the air.

The Narzat stood, balanced on one outstretched branch and opened his arms wide.

"Ga – da!" he exclaimed. He tilted his head and made a splashing gesture at his face.

"He's asking if you're thirsty," whispered the Chirper.

"Oh – yes! Yes I am!" Polly beamed.

The Chirper gestured for her to follow him – carefully – as he paced closer to the centre of the tree. The leaves seemed to dip inward, creating a small pool of water within them. The Narzat broke off a smaller leaf, twisted it delicately into a cup and leaned forward. Polly was surprised as this fearless creature seemed to creep with the utmost caution towards the water – as if he were petrified of falling in. Carefully, he scooped up a cupful and shuffled over to Polly.

"Ghee!" he proudly exclaimed.

"Oh – oh thank you!" she smiled, sitting down in the sun on a branch and sipping the cool liquid. It soothed her dry throat and had a sweetness to it that she couldn't quite unpick.

"Ah! Where have *you* been then?" cawed the Chirper, glaring towards Polly.

Before she could answer, something scurried over her foot. It shivered up her leg, and balanced on her outstretched knee. A tiny reptile, with beautiful blue markings down her back, stood staring at her with hands on its hips. The Looky Lizard tilted her head – inspecting Polly in a way that was firm yet kind – and proceeded to make several gestures at the startled maid. When Polly did not respond, the Lizard turned round and repeated the gestures at the Chatty Chirper.

"This is our friend Looky," he announced. "She says that she... well that's rude! She *dislikes* humans... but you seem OK."

Looky the Lizard turned to face Polly, hands on hips.

"That's a fair point based on who you've met already! I promise you not everyone's like the Snides... I'm Polly. How do you do?" She offered a hand. "Back home, sometimes we shake hands to say hello. And that we want to be friends."

116

The Looky Lizard tilted her head again, slowly took one of Polly's fingers in both hands and shook it.

"And where have you been then?" repeated the Chirper. The Looky Lizard, mischief glinting, stood proudly in front of them. She acted out precisely where she had been. They listened enraptured (the Chirper translating for Polly) by the story of Lord Snide's idiocy, his frustration – and they all shook with laughter at the thought of Lady Snide landing face down in the dirt.

The Chirper then recounted their latest adventure – the Narzat rescuing Polly from the snap-snap dragon, her kind words used to save him – all to approving nods from the Looky Lizard.

"But what I really, really want to know," chirped the Chatty

Chirper, "is precisely how someone like *you* ended up working with someone like *them*?"

Polly smiled, that sad glint in her eyes, and placed her cup down. The Narzat crawled closer and sat down next to her, the Looky Lizard now reclining on his shoulder as they prepared to listen.

"My family has always worked for their family," Polly began. "My father was a butler, my mother was a gardener, and they looked after Snide Mansion well. Of course, it was all owned by Lord Snide's mother... the original Lady Snide. And she was a wonderful person. She always used to insist we join them at Christmas, or share happy stories and smiles whenever she saw us. When I was very little, my parents were taken from me in a horrible accident and... I had no one. Lady Snide – Margaret, she asked me to call her – took me in. I was working as a maid at that point but she didn't make me do a lot of work. Instead, she would play games with me or teach me things. At the age of 6, I knew all the countries in the world and I could do big calculations in my head. At the age of 7, I knew all the Kings and Queens of England, and I knew how to change a tyre and ride a bike. Sometimes, we would play chess, or cards (Double Rummy was her favourite) but best of all, she would read to me.

"Oh! The places she took me in those stories.... They were beyond my imagination. We sailed with pirates, and landed on the moon and I even learnt about the Jumble Jungle Wood! My favourite story of course was *Tarzan* and she would read to me about his adventures again and again.

"I loved that book so much... Margaret surprised me once. She had been teaching me how to cut letters out of wood, and I carved out all the letters to spell 'Tarzan'. One day, she called me into her study.

She'd bought me a great big toy chest, a bulky thing painted green. But she had stuck my 'Tarzan' letters on it. She said to me that it was mine. I was like one of her children and she wanted me to have happy memories playing with it. And that one day, I could even share it with my own children."

Polly's voice trembled and a tear raced to her eye. "It was a good life."

She paused, and steadied herself. The Narzat shuffled closer and she continued.

"Of course, good things don't last long for me. That sweet woman passed away and her son – that foul man who never called or visited – moved in with his foul wife. And my life became one of orders and insults. I was their maid and that was that."

The Looky Lizard looked down for a moment, then signed something to Polly. The Chirper nodded sagely.

"Why did you hang around?"

"Well... I had two reasons. The first was that I made a promise to Margaret. She said to care for her home, and to look after her family. The second reason was that when I was old enough to finally move away and confident enough to move on, I had another

priority. Something else very important was there and I couldn't go fussing about myself then…"

Tears started to well in her eyes. That sadness had bubbled over. The Chirper found himself reduced to single words.

"What?"

"Oh… I can't talk about it. Not yet. I will only cry and we'll never get anywhere! Perhaps, I can tell you more… tomorrow?"

The Narzat nodded. He liked that word. He gestured for Polly to follow him carefully along the tree tops. They reached a large bough where huge wisps of flower branched like mist. The petals swirled and fluffed, looking like clouds. Delicately, the Narzat picked one and passed it to Polly. He passed another to Chirper, one for Looky, and took one for himself.

Carefully, he guided Polly's hand holding the *cloud flower*, and used it to catch the tears that had formed in her eyes. He then turned and whispered something into his own bouquet.

He held up a hand and waited. A gentle breeze was moving towards them across the tree tops, causing the leaves to shimmer.

The Narzat held out his flower and seemed to count to three.

"Gar. Nar. Gee!" He released the petal and watched it float up into the air. The Looky and Chirper did the same, so Polly followed suit. The cloud flowers – carrying Polly's tears and all of their worries – drifted towards the smiling beams of the sun.

They stood there for a moment, enjoying the peace that can only be shared between true friends. Finally, the calm silence was sliced by a horrible shard of reality.

"I'll need to go back," Polly whispered. "The Snides will come looking for me otherwise... But please – can I find you tomorrow?"

The Looky Lizard placed a reassuring hand on Polly's foot, looked up at her and grinned. She moved her other hand, crossing her heart, so there was no mistaking her message.

Polly... we will find you.

Chapter 13

Polly Takes a Trip

Polly arrived back at the camp, a skip in her step and a spring in her heart. She danced round the fire, and flew past the Snides like a sunbeam.

Lord Snide was busy polishing his gun – his forehead creased and a large tongue sticking out the side of his mouth. His fingers itched over the

trigger as he looked up at Polly and then to his wife.

"What's she so happy about?" he snapped.

Lady Snide barely looked up. She was clutching a mirror in one hand, and a tiny bird in the other. Holding the poor creature above her, she viciously squeezed it until tears poured from its eyes and plopped on to her cheeks. Extending a bony finger, she ferociously rubbed the tears into a small blemish, sneering as she did so. Satisfied that the bird could cry no longer, she threw it over her shoulder. It hopped away, exhausted.

"Oi!" boomed Lord Snide. "When you've quite finished beautifying... what's that damned maid so happy about?"

Lady Snide sighed.

"What?"

"That maid... bounding back... grinning, and with no water!" Lord Snide thundered, pointing a sausage finger at Polly's tent.

The Snides glowered at one another, and steered their combined ire towards the tent. Their voices united in one scream: "POLLY!"

Polly poked her head out of her tent, smiling. Questions flew at her like arrows.

"Why are you smiling?"

"Where's the water?"

"What took you so long?"

"Who said you could smile?"

Polly paused. She did not want to reveal her new friends to the Snides, and she needed to find them tomorrow – on her own. Before she'd left the Narzat, Chirper and Looky, she had concocted a plan to get rid of the Lord and Lady.

"Oh... I'm so sorry... it's just that I think I found the treasure... but I'm so sorry about the water! Right – best set off again to get it! See you later!" she blurted, picking up the wash bucket and setting off for the treeline.

"No – no! Wait! Wait!" stormed Lord Snide, scurrying to keep up with her. "What? Where was the treasure?"

Polly paused, again. The Looky Lizard had suggested sending them towards the snap-snap dragon, but Polly

pointed out that that would have been far too cruel. Instead, they had opted for something less hazardous but far more tedious.

"It's not far. You keep walking straight ahead that way until you reach a clear stream," she pointed at a random direction into the jungle. "It didn't look too deep but I was certain that I could see a glint of gold within it."

"Then why didn't you go in?" sneered Lady Snide.

"Well... I can't swim. Remember – you stopped me doing my lessons when I was little," replied Polly.

The Snides paused for a moment, their frowning faces silently battling who should go in the water.

"Well – take us there now!" barked Lady Snide.

"The thing is... it'll be dark by the time we get there. We can go at first light tomorrow?" suggested Polly.

"Fine. Fine," grumbled Lord Snide. "You can wake us up and take us there tomorrow!"

"By all means," smiled Polly, bowing low. Theatrically, she paused and scratched her head. The final part of the plan was due. "Of course, it does mean we won't eat tomorrow night – if that's OK with you both… with us all walking that way, it means no one will be around to cook and prepare dinner."

Lord Snide let out a horrified gasp. Pausing, he scratched his head and finally suggested an idea. Little did he realise it was someone else's idea.

"Lady Snide and I will go tomorrow. You will prepare the meals for the evening. And we will celebrate because *we will have the treasure!*"

"Wait…" barked Lady Snide, holding up her hand and talking past her maid. "Polly isn't exactly the brightest spark. How can she be even sure that she saw the treasure?"

Polly was ready for this. Ignoring that she'd been ignored, she bounded over to a collection of papers, spread out on a makeshift desk.

"Look at this map…. Although no one's ever managed to truly sketch out the layout of the Jumble Jungle Wood, we can see how the Mighty Confused River flows in from the ocean, and through the Three-Headed Mountain. Loads of streams branch off from it.

"We lost the treasure all those years ago, when we were at sea. It stands to reason that it's flowed through the river, floated along here… and ended up in the stream I saw today!"

Lady Snide loomed over her.

"Let's be clear... we didn't lose the treasure. You did," she sneered.

"That doesn't matter," interrupted Lord Snide gleefully. "It'll be ours again soon enough!"

He chuckled and rubbed his hands gleefully together. He loved it when a plan came together.

Fortunately, so did Polly.

***

And so it was the next morning the Snides departed from the camp. Lady Snide put on her finest evening gloves so she would not have to touch any revolting creatures, and Lord Snide clutched his gun in both hands. On his back was a large wooden box, strapped carefully, and containing something he proudly referred to as "his secret weapon".

The Snides set off, leaving Polly to sweep and clean, and polish and dust. She was feeling excited and couldn't stop singing a haunting and beautiful song that just came to her from deep inside.

The Narzat, Looky Lizard and Chatty Chirper arrived on the edge of the camp. The bird and reptile strolled forward but the Narzat remained rooted to the spot. Polly seemed to be singing a memory – her song was a melody of happiness, and hellos, and hugs. The Chirper, blissfully unaware as always, interrupted.

"Lovely tune! I do enjoy a singsong myself – I've been told I can sing lots of different notes in very interesting mixtures! Here let me sing one for you... Hugmmmph!" he began, but the Looky Lizard clamped a hand around his beak before he could begin.

The Narzat bounded forward, standing happily in front of Polly. He shielded his eyes from the sun as he looked up, and grinned. Before Polly even had time to smile back, he had grabbed her hand and started bounding towards the treeline.

They sprinted and sprang, skipping over the branches of upside-down trees, pushing through leaves and vines – the world turning into a blur of green. The Looky Lizard happily rode on Polly's shoulder, all whilst the Chatty Chirper cantered along saying how he'd wished he'd taken up jogging as a pastime. After a short while, the friends stumbled upon their destination… the Jumble Jungle Wood Café.

Polly had never seen anything as beautiful as the Diamond Waterfall, or anything as majestic as the Dark Lake beneath it. The sheer variety and beauty of the different animals was awesome. Giggly mockodiles swapped jokes with *spotted zebras*, whilst bright green dandylions tried to stop their manes blowing away in the wind. Chattermonkeys dove into soda streams, and grumpuses reclined gloomily in bubbling mud pools. Just as Polly was taking in the view, she had to jump backwards as a hulking bear thundered past her. Well, at least she thought it was a bear – she could have mistaken it for a giant fuzz of brown fur. It stood at almost double her height, and triple her width. As the bear brushed past her, Polly couldn't resist stroking its velvety hair. The creature whirled round and growled.

"Oh! Don't mind her! This is a Polly!" excused the Chirper. He whispered to Polly, "This is the Big Brown Boogaloo… He's incredibly cuddly but is rather self-conscious about it."

The Boogaloo sniffed, and trotted over to a warm

pond of steaming water. Pinching his nose, he dived in, leaving bubbles on the surface. A split second passed before a growl filled the air and the Big Brown Boogaloo climbed out of the water – at almost a quarter of the size! His glistening fur hung off him, revealing a long, lank body underneath. Polly stifled a laugh. It looked like someone had hung wet hair on a stick man in order to dry it out.

A group of happy PenGrins waddled by, and Polly couldn't imagine seeing happier animals. Their bright yellow feathers reminded her of sunshine, and their flippers seemed to applaud as they walked. But it was the smile of the PenGrin which struck her. Their wide, purple beaks spread across their faces, showing beaming white teeth and a smile that danced up into their eyes.

Polly surveyed the dozens and dozens of creatures bathing in the various waters, and noticed how curiously empty the Dark Pool was.

"Why doesn't anyone swim in there?" she asked.

"Many reasons… It's far too deep; the weeds will strangle you; you'd probably die… And I hear it's quite nippy this time of year!" chirped the Chirper. "Besides, we're not here to swim… we are here to eat!"

They swept up the stairs into the café. Polly went to sit down on a particularly comfortable looking rock.

"No! That seat's taken!" growled Pertinax's voice from across the hubbub of the café.

"By who?" asked Polly.

"It's reserved for the Polar Where," snapped Pertinax angrily, slamming a pan on the counter.

"Doesn't he mean a polar bear," whispered Polly, glancing around.

"Oh no," explained the Chatty Chirper happily.

"It's the Polar Where. He's a massive blue bear, but no-one can ever seem to find him."

"Isn't that him?" asked Polly, pointing a puzzled finger at a hulking creature, whose furry shoulders seemed to brush against the high ceiling.

"Oh no!" chuckled the Chatty Chirper. "That's the Polar There. She's always wherever you look for her."

They found an inviting stone table with wooden chairs. Pertinax greeted them all with his usual level of grumpy hospitality. He seemed utterly unfazed by the sight of a human, and lumbered over to the stone table where they were sitting. Hearing about Polly saving the Chirper, he reluctantly agreed for her to enjoy a lunch there.

After much clattering of plates and pans, he arrived and spread out a sumptuous spread – there were square-pear smoothies, a quango casserole, sour potato pie, rockand rolls, and baked bug trifle. And that was just for starters.

The friends smiled through their courses, laughing and joking, as they chewed and chattered. The Narzat enjoyed showing off how much food he could fit in his mouth at once, or the impressive

volume of his belches. The Looky Lizard animatedly gestured, telling and retelling more and more stories, occasionally pausing to throw a piece of fruit in the air and catch it in her mouth. Polly could not believe the stories she was hearing. The tale of how the Narzat had once rode on the back of a *velcro vulture*, or how the Chirper had ended up talking to a pack of *vicious nightgrowlers* for so long that they fell asleep. She gasped and wept when the Looky Lizard told her about how she'd lost her family, and applauded at the tale of how she once led a whole group of *do-dodos* to safety in the middle of a storm. The Narzat mimed and growled a retelling of how he'd once eaten a coconut the size of his head, and the Chirper demonstrated how he could name every type of berry in the jungle.

When their plates were empty, their bodies were full of pleasant aches – their stomachs bursting from being too full, and their faces sore from smiling. Pertinax lumbered past, and Polly turned to him.

"That was, without a doubt, the most incredible meal I've ever eaten. Thank you. You're very talented," she said.

Pertinax looked at the floor, mumbled something

embarrassed, and lumbered away. His walk was different to normal though – it seemed that his step bounced more than usual.

"Oh – I say! How about a bit of after dinner entertainment? ShallIsingusasong! I'vegotagoodone!" grinned the Chatty Chirper. The Narzat desperately tried grabbing at the bird's beak, but he missed as the Chatty Chirper proudly strutted out on to the table. His singing began, and it sounded rather like an orchestra where every instrument is broken. The song, needless to say, was so full of

such high-pitched screeches and hideous squawks that all the animals in the café started groaning and shouting for him to stop. The Narzat grabbed some mud from his hair and covered his ears, Pertinax started to smash plates just to drown out the noise, and at a nearby table a school of tree cod dived into their soup. Even poor Polly, so keen to be kind to her friends, had to scrunch up her face and try to cover her ears. In fact, the only person who appeared to be contentedly ignoring the singing was the Looky Lizard. She stretched out on the table, watching the Chirper with a grin on her face.

"Sorry to interrupt," trembled Polly (although, truly she wasn't – her voice stopped the Chirper's singing after all), "But, Looky, I can't help noticing how you seemed to be enjoying the Chirper's song far more than everyone else…"

The Looky Lizard looked at Polly and flashed a mischievous grin. She signed a simple message.

That's because I don't hear.

Indeed, this is true. Hearing is something that the Looky Lizard simply doesn't – or can't – do.

Of course, this was not something the Looky Lizard needed to mention right away. You're

140

probably wondering why I didn't tell you this when I introduced her. The reason is that the Looky Lizard's inability to hear is the least interesting detail about her. I mean – do you go round introducing yourself by saying all the things you can't do? Do you walk up to a new friend and say, "Hello! How are you? I can't smell colour!"? Or do you declare to your teacher: "Did you know I can't taste Roman numerals?" There are a thousand and one things that the Looky Lizard *can* do (such as glow in the dark, read lips and beaks, talk by using her hands, sense voices and movement through vibrations) and these are far more impressive than the simple fact that she does not hear.

And, regardless of her hearing, the Looky Lizard was probably the best listener that ever there was.

Polly? she danced *What's the matter?*

"Matter?" said Polly with a perplexed frown.

The Looky Lizard stepped forward and tilted her head to one side.

You have tears waiting. Please don't hide them.

Polly glanced out of the café window, through the falling waterfall, and realised that her eyes were indeed glistening again with her secret sadness. Yet, for the first time in her life, this sadness had not gone

unmarked – for her three friends were next to her. All at once, in their own ways, they asked the same question.

The Looky Lizard placed a hand on Polly's shoulder.

"Gyarn?" growled the Narzat sympathetically.

"Are you alright? Is it wind?" squawked the Chirper.

"No... no... it's not that..." chuckled Polly. "It's just that I've not been entirely honest with you. About why I've really stuck with the Snides over the last few years. I stayed with them because I needed to get here. And now I'm here, I need your help."

The three friends nodded. Polly took a deep breath.

"Several years ago, the Snides decided they wanted to sail around the world. They bought the biggest, most expensive yacht possible and off they went. Of course, they did none of the work. They had sailors to sail, cooks to cook, and me to do the rest of the work. We were at sea for months... but I didn't mind because... because... I had my child with me."

The Looky and the Chirper exchanged a gasp, and the Narzat cupped his head in his hands. Polly continued.

"My little boy. He was perfect, and he was only little – just about to turn three. We would get up every day to watch the sunrise over the water. We would fish together, or spot shapes from the clouds, or sing to each other. It was marvellous. Of course, I had to hide him away from the temper of Lord and Lady Snide – when they were about, I'd take him below deck to play with the special toy chest that Margaret had given me.

"One of those days, he found something in the toy chest, wedged right at the bottom. It was a letter from Margaret and it said on the front… 'For my son, and the daughter I wish was mine, Lord Snide and Polly.'

"As much as I wanted, I couldn't open a letter with someone else's name on it! I went looking for Lord Snide but I found the Lady instead. She snatched the letter off

me and
ripped it
open. I still
remember her
face as she read it – more
angry, more sharp than usual –
but she never let me have a look."

"Did you ever find out what it said?" squawked the Chirper.

"No. I was going to ask... but I became distracted because it was my boy's 3rd birthday the next day! I wanted it to be special. That night, I hoisted the toy chest up on to deck – we were going to play a game as soon as the sun rose – and asked the cooks to secretly bake a cake for him. I couldn't afford a present, but I had a special necklace that Margaret had given me and I hid it in the box especially. I went to bed, kissed him goodnight and sang him to sleep. And that... and that was the last time I saw him."

Silence. A tear rolled down the Chirper's cheek. Polly buried her face in her hands. Her voice became delicate, ready to break at any second.

"Later that night, there was a terrible storm. I was awoken by thunder and could tell something was wrong. I got up to check on him – but he wasn't in his bed. I ran up on to the deck and – and the toy chest was gone. Lady Snide said she saw him playing with it. She said we could assume that a wave came and swept them both overboard."

Her shoulders were shaking now. The Narzat climbed over the table and hugged her, whilst the Looky Lizard cradled her hand. The Chirper sobbed, and blew his beak into a half-eaten trifle. Polly stared out through the waterfall, tears streaming down her face.

"The thing I miss most is holding his hand. When he was very little, he would hold my hand all the time because he needed to... because a step was too big, or he wanted to show me something. But he didn't need to do that as much as he got bigger. When he held my hand, it was because he wanted to. When he held my hand, it was like saying – 'Mum, I love you and want to be close'. Oh – I would give everything to hold his hand for just one second more!"

That secret sadness that had always lurked in Polly's eyes had made its way free, and sorrow shone from her face.

"Is that why you're here?" growled a voice. Pertinax

was now standing at her table, the rest of the café listening to her in silence.

"Yes," she nodded, glancing at her new audience. "Turns out the Snides need that necklace. Apparently it's really valuable to them. They've been looking for it for years, and they've realised that it must have washed up somewhere in the Jumble Jungle Wood and I hope that – I *pray* that – that my son is somewhere here too. So, what I'm asking is that, if… if you can… if you don't mind…"

"We'll help you find him," soothed the Chatty Chirper.

"We'll all help you," rumbled Pertinax.

"Garg," growled the Narzat.

Chapter 14

Snides Go Exploring

Lord and Lady Snide lumbered through the jungle, bickering and barking. She felt he walked too slowly whereas he felt she walked too fast. She thought he was a big buffoon whereas he felt she was a vile harpy. He grunted insults and she screeched swear words. As they walked, trees recoiled their vines, bugs scurried away and birds swooped off into the distance.

After an hour or more, the ground beneath them became distinctly softer, and softer still, until they were wading through thick mud. Unlike the usual mud that you can just knock off your boots, this dirt clung to their legs and clung to their clothes, staining Lady Snide's pristine white dress all sorts of colours as she squelched along. She was about to fire off another round of her most spectacular insults, when something caught her eye.

Ahead of them, a stream flowed gently along – just as Polly had promised them. It was crystal clear, and you could peer through to the very bottom as easily as looking through a window. The Snides edged forward to get a closer look. Beneath the glassy surface, rocks glistened in the sunlight, and mysterious shapes darted about. Peering closer, the Snides realised those shapes were *glassfish*, whose see-through scales cut delicate outlines in the water.

A distant roar – or was it a scream? – caused them to look up. On the other side of the water, a dark tangle of thorns and creaking trees loomed. Shadows danced around dying branches. The world seemed to grow indescribably darker within that part of the jungle, and dark shapes moved, cracking twigs and scraping against the trees. Far above those tree tops, grey clouds swirled. The Snides did not know that this area beyond the stream was the very edge of the Deep Dark Depths. But they were certain they did not want to venture any further. Their eyes returned to the water.

"How deep is it?" murmured Lady Snide. Lord Snide shrugged, picked up a muddy rock and threw it in. As the stone sank, the dirt seemed to leap off it and float to the sides of the stream – it was as if the water could not bear to have any mud within it. Lord Snide rubbed his chin.

"Looks deep," he mused. "Are you going in?"

Lady Snide raised one eyebrow.

"Fine," Lord Snide muttered. "I have a better plan, anyway…" He reached for the box on his back and pulled it down. It proudly stated "TNT" on the side of it. Reaching in, he grabbed a stick of dynamite.

"All we need to do is blow that thing out of the water! I light this, throw it in… and 'boom!' If the treasure is there, it'll jump out of the stream!"

Lord Snide grinned – a smile that was wiped off his face when Lady Snide shoved him backward into the mud.

"Dunderhead! What if you break the treasure?!"

"Umm… well…"

"In your mother's letter, it said two things very clearly… The first was that the necklace isn't just a

necklace... She said it was the most priceless piece of treasure that she possessed! That batty old sow owned lots of precious things... goodness knows how much it is worth! And you want to use dynamite to get it? Oaf!"

Lord Snide glared up at his wife, and realised he

did not have a retort. Instead, he angrily fired his gun into the stream, hoping to hit a glassfish. He could not tell if he succeeded.

After much further arguing – with several swear words and even more insults – it was agreed that Lord Snide would have to search through the stream himself. Grumbling, he lowered himself down the bank and plunged into the coldness. The water came up to his knees, then his waist, as he began to wade. Kicking at rocks, he stroked his chins as he stumbled.

A loud *plop* sounded behind Lord Snide, sending ripples towards him. He whirled round to see a huge frog poking its head above the surface. Its vivid green face could only be described as two large eyes, and an even larger grin. The frog raised a webbed foot and waved enthusiastically.

What to do when met with such a friendly greeting? Lord Snide roared, lifted his gun and pointed at the creature. He pulled the trigger.

As water erupted behind it, the frog darted below the surface and swam behind Lord Snide. Poking its head out again, the amphibian pointed up at the box on Lord Snide's back and, in a tuneful voice, began to read.

"Tuh... Nuh.. Tuh... TunNuhTuh!" it chortled, pointing at the letters TNT. Lord Snide heard a horrendous cracking noise behind him – it was his wife laughing.

"Oh! How marvellous!" she cried as she clapped her hands together. "It's a PhonoFrog – I've heard all about them. They love nothing more than to read, and say hello!"

As if to confirm this, the PhonoFrog pointed at the lettering on Lord Snide's box and chortled again.

"TerNerTer! Ternerter! Ternerter!" it laughed, before continuing, "H – igh – ly... Highly!"

The frog paused, scratched its chin whilst puzzling out the final word. "Explosive! Explosive!"

"Where did you read about these?" demanded Lord Snide.

"Oh – in one of my magazines. Apparently, if you mash them up well enough they make a delightful shampoo!" she laughed.

Lord Snide raised his gun and pointed it at the frog.

"I'll give you 'highly explosive' !" he growled.

"Wait!" shouted Lady Snide, rushing down the bank and into the water. She grasped her husband's shoulders.

"Let me shoot this damned toad!" he demanded.

"It's a frog! And shut up!" Lady Snide exclaimed. "There's something we've missed! Polly didn't bring any water back... Why?"

Lord Snide shook his head as she continued.

"And she said she didn't look in the stream because she can't swim... but it's only knee deep!"

Lord Snide looked dumbfounded. Lady Snide glanced at the PhonoFrog, and with a sudden lunge grabbed it round its neck.

"You! Did you see some wild-haired, ridiculous woman here yesterday?"

"Turnurtur. Highly explosive," the frog croaked, shaking its head vigorously. Lady Snide cast the poor creature back into the water where it promptly swam away. She glared at her husband.

"She lied to us! She never came here... Which means... she's keeping us out of the way! She's got a secret and we need to find out what it is! Come – let's find that brat!"

With a scurry, the Snides started wading through the mud, back towards their camp. And back towards Polly.

Chapter 15

Attack of the Hug-a-Slugs

"This is wonderful!" declared Polly, as she lay in a leaf-hammock surrounded by Hug-a-Slugs. After fond farewells at the Jumble Jungle Wood Café, her friends had walked her back towards the camp. It had been agreed that they would unite search parties in the morning and go looking for her son from there. Polly would have started immediately if she didn't have to get back for Lord and Lady Snide.

However, as they had lumbered through the jungle, the Narzat couldn't resist one bit of fun. He led Polly, Looky and the Chirper through a gap in the trees and to the Hug-a-grove. The Chirper squawked his concern that they would be late back, but the

Looky Lizard calmly pointed out that they were only a hop, skip and a jump from the camp... and that he was a cowardly idiot who could do with shutting up, thank you.

Polly could not contain her smiles at the sight of the Hug-a- Slugs. They had fluffily flocked towards her, purring and cooing with fascination at the sight of a human. A bright blue one managed to launch itself off a particularly springy shrub and land into Polly's arms. It cooed, waving its antenna, as she cuddled it. The Narzat waved her over to a hammock, and Polly found herself reclining happily in the leaf with a crowd of Hug-a-Slugs.

As she lay there, surrounded by fluff and cuddles, she noticed a strange feeling. It was almost across her shoulders, almost in her stomach, and almost everywhere for that matter. That secret sadness felt different. Oh – the sorrow still lurked, still hurt, but she felt lighter. It was a secret no longer, and having friends to help her carry it meant that she felt a little bit better.

The Narzat watched her, grinning happily. He had always loved smiles – and he preferred other people's to his own – but Polly's was his very favourite. It stirred memories of happy times, and something deeper than friendship.

"Ooh! Ooh! Not so tickly! Hoo hoo hoo!" the Chirper chortled as a pair of baby Hug-a-Slugs chased each other over his toes. The Looky Lizard, buried in the green fur of a nearby slug, poked her head up and gave an amused shake of her head.

The Narzat sniggered, and began to clap his hands together, telling Polly in a series of grunts and growls about why he loved this area.

"Grrag shmar! Grrrr ragarag, ree gar? Re – row!" he growled.

Polly was so engrossed in the conversation that she did not hear the heavy footsteps behind her. She did not hear the laboured panting of a large man who'd just traipsed through the jungle, or that familiar tut of disgust from a human icicle.

Lord and Lady Snide stepped forward together, surveying the scene. There was something quite frankly distasteful about the amount of joy on show. Lord Snide spotted the Chirper and began to reach for his gun.

The Narzat glanced up and noticed that horrible man from before, pointing the boomy-stick at his friend. With a roar, he leapt up, squeezing a Hug-a-Slug with all his might. The bug whooped and whirred, slime beginning to ooze through its fur. It flew from the Narzat's grip and smacked Lord Snide in the face.

With the sudden commotion, Polly jumped out of her hammock, falling at the feet of Lady Snide who grabbed Polly's arm, digging her jagged fingernails into her flesh.

Meanwhile, Lord Snide roared, whirling round to point the gun at the Narzat. The Narzat fired another Hug-a-Slug back at him. The Looky Lizard followed suit, squeezing her slug so hard that it launched straight at Lord Snide's stomach (which was quite an easy target, in fairness). Soon the air was full of flying Hug-a-Slugs that were happily pelting and belting Lord Snide all over.

Lord Snide would not be bested by these darned animals, and fired his gun blindly at them. The bullet whizzed through the air, scraping just above the Narzat's shoulder. It tore away a large chunk of mud, exposing a glint of metal. Lady Snide's eyes widened as she pulled Polly from the floor.

"Come on! Come on! Let's go!" squawked the Chirper, swooping at his friends and wildly ushering them away.

"Grraga!" roared the Narzat.

"We'll find her tomorrow!" pecked the bird as he pushed his friends away.

Polly looked up, just in time to see the Looky Lizard signal – *Jumble Jungle Wood Café, tomorrow* – before the three friends vanished into the trees. The poor maid was left with nothing but the misery of the Snides as she climbed back to her feet.

"Back to camp. Now," growled Lord Snide, a face of thunder as he pointed away from the clearing. He turned and kicked a Hug-a-Slug, before storming off. Polly slunk after him.

Lady Snide paused, thinking – or should I say scheming? She had seen something on that strange creature's neck. And she was certain it was the necklace.

***

Polly sat down in front of the campfire, arms shaking, as Lord Snide paced up and down in front of her. She had been hoping to distract the Snides again tomorrow, but now that plan was in trouble. In fact, her very friends were in trouble if the Lord and Lady found them.

"You lied – *lied* – about the necklace! You didn't go to that stream! Instead, you were off cavorting with those... those monsters!" growled Lord Snide.

Polly opened her mouth, but Lady Snide spoke before she could.

"Husband dear," she purred in a voice as sweet as poison, "Perhaps... perhaps we were looking in the wrong place. Are you sure you followed Polly's directions exactly?"

Lord Snide looked at her aghast – so many expletives and curse words were trying to leave his mouth at once that his jaw had remained jammed open. Polly's eyes flickered to Lady Snide. What was going on?

"And Polly... did you have any idea that there were those strange creatures around you?" continued Lady Snide.

Polly's mind raced.

"Um... no. What creatures? You see... I was just looking for... your dinner! When I found those cuddly slug things. I thought that they'd be great for your skin care so I was just trying them out when... when you showed up! What creatures, sorry?"

"See. She had *no* idea," clapped Lady Snide.

"NO IDEA?!" roared Lord Snide.

"No idea... about what?" chimed in Polly.

Lord Snide was about to boom louder than his gun ever had but Lady Snide calmly placed her fist in his mouth, silencing him.

"So... tomorrow, we'll go looking again. Polly – I expect you to have this camp in perfect condition for our return. We may be gone even longer so there will be no excuses. Now, off to your tent," she sneered, waving her hand.

Polly curtsied, and scurried off to her tent. She could not believe her luck.

Polly *should not* have believed her luck. Lady Snide released her husband's mouth, turning to whisper in his ear.

"That creature... that friend of hers... was wearing the necklace!"

"What!?"

"Shh! Be quiet, you big fool. Polly would never tell us what that *beast* is... but she can lead us to it. Nod if you understand."

Lord Snide nodded, a devious grin spreading across his face.

"So tomorrow… we'll pretend to leave camp, then we'll double back and follow Polly. She'll lead us straight to that creature. And to that necklace!"

Lord Snide grinned and lovingly reached for the TNT box on his back.

"An almost perfect plan… what will we do with the creature? And that damned bird?"

"Oh Lord Snide… you can shoot them both for all I care."

The camp rang with the hideous sound of their cruel laughter.

Chapter 16

The Perfect Plan

Polly was surprisingly easy to follow.

The Snides had left that morning, noisily shouting orders and goodbyes. As soon as they had disappeared behind some trees, they hid and watched Polly.

The maid was skittishly dancing round the camp, doing her usual chores, and checking the grandfather clock that the Snides had insisted on bringing. After 5 minutes, she quickly departed into the jungle. The Snides stalked after her, ferocious predators tracking their prey.

So excited was Polly at the thought of seeing her friends, and having a whole team of animals helping her to find her son, that she did not look back – not once. If only she had glanced over her shoulder here, or paused to turn there, she would have seen that vile Lord and Lady ducking and diving behind trees.

But the Jumble Jungle Wood Café beckoned.

Polly had no idea about who had followed her. As she arrived, she waved to the Brown Boogaloo Bear, and danced around a dandylion. All the animals were assembled there (well, the helpful ones at least) – they'd heard tale of poor Polly's plight and they were keen to help. A retractable giraffe extended its neck in a friendly nod as she passed, and a mockodile gave a friendly grin.

Polly walked round the Dark Lake, darted up the steps that wound up the cliff face and behind the waterfall, and through to the Jumble Jungle Wood Café.

The Chirper was waiting for her there, with a steaming pile of ohmygoshages (like sausages, but even more surprising).

"Morning!" he beamed.

"Morning Chirper! Where's the Narzat?" she replied.

"Oh – he and Looky are working on a surprise for you… they said to meet you here and they wouldn't be long! You must be starving. Would you like an osh my goshage?"

"What surprise?" chuckled Polly.

"They wouldn't tell me – apparently I'm no good with secrets! I reckon it's a nice picture though. Ooh! Shouldn't have said that!" he clamped his wings over his beak. The Narzat and the Looky Lizard were indeed making a nice picture. They had got up at sunrise and ripped some bark off a tree, and had spent the next few hours painting with the colour rushes that lined the banks of the inky river. The Chirper had two jobs: keep the picture a secret, and entertain Polly at the café. He had only succeeded in the latter.

Polly took a bite out of an ohmygoshage and a smile surprised her face.

"Half the jungle's out there for you," rumbled a voice as Pertinax lumbered over to their table. "I reckon you'll find your boy in no time."

Pertinax attempted a smile, but found it hurt his

cheeks in quite an unpleasant way, so he returned to frowning and twiddled his eyebrows.

BANG!

A gunshot pierced the air.

"What's that?" cried Pertinax.

"It sounds like the boom-stick! And it came from out there!" squawked Chirper.

Hearts thumping, they ran to the entrance of the Jumble Jungle Wood Café, and looked down the steps to the bottom of the cliff. A terrible sight greeted them.

Lord Snide was standing, gun smoking, with his foot astride a box of dynamite. All the animals had been

rounded up, and were huddling together in a giant group. Lady Snide walked amongst them, poking each one in turn and shaking her head. Her glittering tiara wobbled as she shook her head angrily.

"It's not you… it's not you… it's not you…" she sneered, shoving and pushing an animal here, or scratching a creature there.

She turned to her husband.

"Have you got enough bullets to shoot them all?" she snarled. He chuckled and tapped his bulging pockets. Several animals whimpered.

"Lord and Lady Snide… What are you doing here?" Polly called down from the entrance of the café.

Lady Snide barely looked up the steps towards Polly. She was stabbing her finger into a retractable giraffe, who had wound his neck into his torso much like a tortoise in its shell. Stepping back, she slowly turned her head and bared her teeth at her maid.

"We are looking for your new friend. Where is he?" demanded Lady Snide.

"Yes… tell us now, or we'll select one of these animals to make a fine fireside rug back home!" bellowed Lord Snide, swinging his gun from side to

side. A pink flamingo turned even white from fear, and a white flamingo turned pink in worry.

The Chirper was not a brave bird. Far from it. Which is what made his next act far more courageous. With a theatrical bow, he started strutting down the steps. His terror at seeing the huge man and the boom stick surged through him, but he managed to hide it with a confident squawk.

"I assume you mean me! I am the Chatty Chirper! Pleased to meet you again," he cawed. He reached the feet of Lady Snide and bowed. "There is no need to bother these fair animals any more, for I am here to – PUKAR!"

Lady Snide snatched him by the throat, and hoisted him into the air. She pushed her face into his, bending his beak with her nose. Her eyes – pools of fury – burned into his.

"You are not what we want. You are nothing. Where is the other creature?" she growled.

The Chirper swallowed down his fear, and replied cooly.

"The Narzat? I won't tell you anything about him. You won't even know his name."

Every single assembled creature groaned and rocked their faces in their palms.

"Where is the Narzat?" shouted Lady Snide up to Polly.

Polly, for once in her life, did not know what to say. She stood, her mouth opening and forming words that would not come. Pertinax placed a hand on her shoulder.

Lord Snide growled impatiently, and raised his gun.

"Oh this is taking too long! I'll just shoot that gorilla next to her!" he bellowed, taking aim.

Polly threw herself in front of Pertinax, spreading her arms wide.

"No! Please! Please don't hurt them!" she called.

Lord Snide did not lower his weapon. His fingers itched on the trigger.

"You have five seconds to tell me where the Narzat is…" shouted Lady Snide. "Or we will be taking a very fine-looking, gorilla-shaped rug back to camp. FIVE."

Lady Snide's voice sliced the silence.

"FOUR!"

Lord Snide squinted some more

"THREE!"

The jungle animals shook uncontrollably.

"TWO!"

Pertinax closed his eyes, and pushed Polly away from him.

"ONE!"

"GUNARG!"

A voice roared in the distance. The Snides, Polly and every animal turned to look across the Dark Lake. Standing on the other side of the water was the Narzat. The Looky Lizard perched on his shoulder. One Narzat hand clutched a small painting, whilst the other was clenched into a fist. His chest rose and fell rapidly, as those deep brown eyes tried to take in the scene before him.

Lady Snide placed a hand delicately on her

husband's gun, and paced to the edge of the Dark Lake. She called across the water.

"Come here, Narzat. We just want to talk. We promise not to hurt you."

All the animals exchanged nervous glances of disbelief.

"This can all be over soon. We just want that necklace of yours…" she shouted as softly as she could.

The Narzat paused. He glanced at the Looky and cupped a hand to his mouth.

"Fuglarg?" he roared

"Um… sorry – may I interject?" flapped the Chirper, whose throat was still in Lady Snide's grip. "He's wondering what a 'necklace' is?"

"The thing I saw around his neck yesterday!" snapped Lady Snide.

"Oh! Neck…lace… Lovely word! Haven't heard it before! Anyway, he calls that his shiny!" grinned the Chirper. He cupped his wings around his beak and cawed across to the Narzat. "She means your shiny! SHINY! They call it a 'neck – lace!'"

The Narzat reached for the locket hanging from his neck. His shiny? This was the necklace they had been looking for all this time? He took a step forward, preparing to go round the lake. The Looky Lizard grabbed his ear, and swung in front of his face, frantically gesturing.

They'll kill you! They're not safe!

"Flarg?" asked the Narzat. What else could he do? They were going to hurt his friends. There was no way out. Or so he thought. The Looky Lizard winked at him – a plan had formed in her mind.

She turned and waved, and flashed her blue scales at the Chirper. The reptile danced and whirled with large, expressive gestures.

Peering from a distance, the Chirper slowly translated for the Snides.

"Umm... they're saying... that he doesn't have the shiny – the neck...lace – with him. It's hidden an hour or so away from here if you want to follow him."

Lord Snide tugged on his moustaches.

"No! No no no no!" he spat, jumping up and down on the ground. "I've had it with this jungle. I'm not going anywhere! NARZAT – You have two hours to bring the necklace to us. Lady Snide will be waiting in the café... with your dear Polly at gunpoint!"

He tossed his rifle to Lady Snide. The animals gasped – at least they were about to go free.

"I will be waiting here – with the other animals. *And* my special box of dynamite!" He tapped the box with his foot.

"Let me dumb that down for you, Narzat," shrieked Lady Snide. "If you are even a second late, Lord Snide

will blow up this menagerie of animals. And if you try *anything* funny… I will get rid of Polly."

She sneered with delight at her husband, who sneered back.

"Don't! Don't!" cried Polly, running down the steps, and pushing past Lady Snide. She waved across the water, waving her hands frantically. "Run away, Narzat! If you do get the necklace for them, they'll shoot you… or eat you… or grind you into makeup!"

Lady Snide yanked Polly by the hair so viciously that she fell. She pointed the rifle at her and gestured for her to go back to the café. Polly stole one miserable glance at her friends across the lake, before climbing to her feet. As Lady Snide pushed and prodded her with the gun up the steps to the café, she called out to Pertinax.

"Gorilla! Join the other animals. If any of you move, bye-bye Polly!"

The other animals remained rooted to the spot as a red-faced Lord Snide pulled out a spool of wire from the box of TNT, his belly shaking with mirth.

Across the lake, the Looky Lizard looked aghast at the Narzat. She had wanted to lead the Snides into the jungle, and lose them along the way. But they had outplayed her. How could they free their friends, without the Narzat meeting a sticky end?

She needed a plan and fast. But before that, she and the Narzat had to get moving. They only had two hours. She grabbed him by the hand and headed into the jungle.

Chapter 17

The Clock is Ticking...

The Narzat and the Looky Lizard ran together, going nowhere but getting there fast. They sprinted through the jungle, past the field of hug-a-slugs and into Camp Snide. They looked round for something – anything to help. There was a desk awash with papers, a dwindling fire, and Lord Snide's chair surrounded by remnants of his breakfast. The Narzat glanced at the peelings of vegetables, the scraps of meat and bones, and growled at the Looky Lizard.

She agreed. That man had an appetite worse than any predator. Well, apart from one.

That's when it hit her. There was one predator

worse than that Snide and, it could provide them with the distraction they needed to rescue everyone.

She turned to the Narzat and quickly signed her plan. He looked at her – frightened but understanding. Her idea was dangerous – impossible perhaps. But there was the slightest chance that it might just work.

***

Outside the Jumble Jungle Wood Café, Lord Snide had gathered all the animals together, crowded around the box of dynamite. Pertinax was amongst them, sitting gloomily next to the Chirper (whose mouth had been tied shut). After much effort, Lord Snide had tied the animals up together, quite ingeniously using a length of wire that ran from the TNT box,

around various animals' legs and arms, and into the large switch box that he sat next to. A simple flick of the switch, and a current would travel along the wire and cause the dynamite box to erupt into the biggest explosion the jungle had ever witnessed. A cruel part of Lord Snide (and that was a very large part of him indeed) secretly hoped the Narzat would be late so he could set it off.

In the café itself, Lady Snide had bound Polly's hands behind her back (using the strings of her apron, no less). The maid sat, despairing, at a table by the edge of the waterfall. Her eyes caught the falling silver of the water. Lady Snide lounged opposite her, keeping the gun trained on Polly in one hand. The other rested on the table, her crimson claws drumming out a sharp rhythm.

Clickety – clack. Clickety – clack.

Polly's trembling voice heaved itself out into the air.

"Please. Please don't hurt them when they get back," she whispered.

Clickety – clack. Clickety – clack.

"They can give you the necklace, and then we can go," Polly hushed again.

Clickety – clack. Clickety – clack.

"Lady Snide, I've – I've never asked for anything – but I'm begging—"

CLICKETY – SMACK!!

Lady Snide slammed her hand on the table, and snarled. Baring her pearly-white fangs, she waved her finger at Polly. It was as if she were searching for the most painful words possible.

"I never liked you," she snarled, her words dripping with disdain.

"I know," replied Polly. She fought back a small chuckle and shook her head. "I know."

Lady Snide stood up, waving the gun at her face.

"Oh, 'you know', do you? I don't like you, Polly. In fact, I detest you. I despise every part of you – from your sad little eyes to your pathetic smile. Do you know why?" she shrieked. Spit flew from her mouth and her voice had reached an even higher pitch of hatred.

Polly looked back, and smiled again. She stayed perfectly still, and leaned forward.

"Lady Snide, in all truthfulness, I don't really care."

"HOW DARE YOU! HOW DARE YOU!" Lady Snide roared, slamming the gun on the table and pinning it with one hand. She clenched her fist and gritted her teeth, searching for the words that would make Polly realise the level of her hatred – the words that would cause her to hurt.

"This… this is all your fault!" she panted. "We have to traipse through this disgusting forest of… muck, dragging you with us, scouring for treasure and… you – YOU – don't even care what I think?"

She trembled in rage, panting and frenzied, staring down at the gun.

"No. I don't," Polly replied. She looked out of the waterfall smiling. "I learnt long ago that your opinions just don't matter. You're not kind. You're obsessed with riches, and looking after yourself and this – this treasure! There's things far more important in life."

"Like *WHAT*?!"

"Brilliant things, full of hope and wonder – things that make your heart sing! Like my friends. And my son."

All at once, Lady Snide grew still. Her breathing slowed and a grin – or was it a grimace? – crept across her face.

"Your son?" she smiled.

"Yes."

"Your son?" Lady Snide was chuckling now.

Polly nodded and spoke clearly.

"You'll never understand that either. You don't know what it is to love someone. How I wish I had held him tight that evening and not let him sneak off to that box and—"

Lady Snide was crying with laughter now. It was a screech, like a hyena, and she pounded the table with her hand. Tears of mirth joined the corners of her eyes. She finally controlled herself and looked at Polly.

"Oh… Polly! This is really quite *delicious!*" she purred. "All these years you've been moping around, thinking that it was your fault your boy disappeared! I guess it was in a manner of speaking…

"*You* showed me the letter from Lord Snide's Mother, or 'Margaret' as you insisted on calling her. You never realised that it was her will. Do you even know what it said?"

Polly shook her head. Lady Snide laughed and continued gleefully.

"It said that when you had a child at the age of three – the same age that Margaret met you – the entire Snide fortune and Snide estate would go to you both. And my husband and I wouldn't have a penny!

"It was the eve of that brat's third birthday and we were about to lose everything! I had to act fast. Oh – how I remember the storm that night! How it rocked the boat so wildly! And how easy it was to wake up your little boy, call him up on to deck, and ask him to climb into the toy box to surprise his mummy. He was so *gullible*. So ignorant of what was going on…"

Polly found herself standing.

"What? No… no!" she whispered.

Oblivious, or simply not caring, Lady Snide charged on.

187

"The funniest thing is that he was laughing when I gave that toy box a push overboard! He had no idea. He barely even screamed when he hit the waves."

"My – my son!" Polly cried. "And you let me think that this was all my fault?! You monster!"

"It is your fault! If you hadn't hidden that damned necklace in that damned toy box, we wouldn't be in this damned situation! SO SIT DOWN!" snarled Lady Snide, prodding Polly so hard that she slumped into her chair.

Lady Snide lowered herself back into her chair, and began tapping the table again.

"So Polly... do you understand now?" she grinned. "I don't like you."

Clickety – clack.

***

Breathless, the Looky Lizard and the Narzat finally reached the clear stream that marked the edge of the Deep Dark Depths. Standing, panting, they stared at how the land seemed to darken on the other side of the glassy water. The darkened trees seemed to wait, clamped together like the jaws of some slumbering beast.

Looky glanced at the Narzat and nodded. She placed a hand over her nose and dived forward into the stream. As she began paddling across, the Narzat remained rooted. His eyes bulged and he shuffled on the spot searching for some other way to cross… there! A short jog down the edge of the water was an overturned tree. It bridged the water, providing a clear – and dry – path across. The Narzat pointed at it and roared to the Looky. She waved a brief thumbs up from the water, and he began sprinting off to the makeshift bridge.

The Looky lizard had barely heaved herself out of the stream on to the other bank when something yanked on her tail. She spun round and saw a large grin and an even larger pair of eyes staring back at her. The PhonoFrog had grasped her tail in a webbed hand. Kicking back at him, and swishing her tail in an aggressive warning, she turned to carry on. With a short grunt, the frog leapt in front of her. Blocking her path, he happily croaked: "Narzat! Nuh – AR – Zuh – Ah – Tuh!"

Looky tilted her head to one side. She had never met this creature before – the Jumble Jungle

Wood was a big place after all – and she was fairly certain the Narzat hadn't either. She should have carried on running, but she found her curiosity causing her to sign a simple question: *How do you know his name?*

The PhonoFrog was surprisingly adept at reading all languages, and most situations, so he beckoned in reply.

"Narzat! Narzat!" he cried, before turning and bounding upstream along the bank. Glancing over her shoulder, the Looky Lizard could see the Narzat had crossed the downed tree and was now sprinting into the Deep Dark depths. Turning her head to the opposite direction, she could see the PhonoFrog urgently waving for her to follow. His expression was so sincere, so full of importance, but she knew that every second counted in helping her friends. But what if that small frog had something vital to tell her? Surely, she could spare a few moments?

She took one glance back at the Narzat, sighed and decided that she had to follow her gut and follow the frog.

**

The Narzat's footsteps hammered across the forest floor. Over the thudding of his heart, and the panting of his breath, he became aware of the deathly silence closing in around him. The sun had disappeared behind the thick knot of branches above him, and roots snaked their way to trip him up.

Pausing, the Narzat looked round. It was time.

"GGRRRRAR!"

He roared at the top of his voice, louder than he had ever roared before, pounding his chest and stamping his feet. He roared until his throat hurt and his lungs felt fit to burst. So fierce, so angry, so defiant was this roar that bats soared from their hiding places and various creepy crawlies crept and crawled away.

The Narzat stood panting, and waiting.

That's when he heard it.

The ground shook and the air quivered. Footsteps thundered closer and closer, before a vicious, hungry snarl shook the air. Bursting through the trees, splintering wood and the silence, stormed the Ravenoserous.

Fury burned within its eyes as its feet pounded upon the earth. Its claws made an awful clickety-clack as it tore over the ground towards the Narzat. The Ravenoserous opened its jaws wide and roared.

The Narzat froze and closed his eyes. The predator was a matter of footsteps away – he could feel the heat of its rank breath swirl. Its jaws were one snap away from closing around him. The Narzat paused a second longer, grabbed a heartbeat's worth of rest and snapped his eyes open. He turned and ran. The first part of the plan was in motion.

***

The PhonoFrog finally stopped by a bend in the water. From here, an even smaller stream had branched off, cutting into the muddy embankment and creating a small pool. The Looky Lizard arrived alongside him and shrugged her shoulders, glancing round. What was she supposed to be looking at?

"Narzat! Narzat!" croaked the frog. He pointed down towards the edge of the water.

Fringing the pool were bushes and bushes dripping with shushberries. Their dark purple fruit seemed to droop seductively towards the water. But this was not what the PhonoFrog was pointing at.

Lying slightly further down the bank, crumbling and splintered, was a box. An old box. A toy box. It had been battered and bruised and weathered and whipped, and it jutted forlornly out of the mud. It looked as though it had crashed into the bank many, many years ago and had remained there ever since.

Lying on the floor next to it was a group of wooden capital letters, all chipped and faded. They barely stood out from the thick dirt beside them and remained jumbled together, spelling out a simple

word. The PhonoFrog pointed at each one in turn, proudly reading them to the Looky Lizard.

"Nuh – Ar – Zuh – Ah – Tuh! Narzat!" he croaked.

As if in a daze, the Looky Lizard wandered over to the letters and picked them up. Cradling them in her arms, she turned back towards the toy box. On its side, she could see on the box a faint outline where they'd once been hammered in. She slowly lined the "N" up with the marking on the box, before swiftly returning each individual letter to its original place. She stepped back, her eyes flitting over the new arrangement of the letters.

They spelt "TARZAN".

Chapter 18

Pulling Together

The Looky Lizard stood staring at the battered box, her mind whirring. Her eyes turned towards the shushberry bushes, and down at herself – caked and covered in mud. A silent gasp escaped her mouth and she caught it with a scaled hand. Nodding in thanks to the frog, the Looky Lizard knew she had to find her friends and tell them about her discovery.

"Narzat! Narzat!" croaked the frog. He hopped up and down and pointed further down the bank.

Turning, the Looky Lizard saw something in the distance – her friend, the Narzat, sprinting towards the stream and jumping over it. He landed with a dull splat on the muddy embankment, the water inches beneath his feet. He scrabbled up, and carried on running.

Seconds after, a roar tore the air, and a blur of fur and teeth bounded over the stream in a single jump in hot pursuit. The Ravenoserous was on the move.

The Looky Lizard paused to hug the frog and took off after them.

**

Alongside the Dark Lake, near to the steps that led up to the Jumble Jungle Wood Café, the animals remained bound together in a circle. Lord Snide remained in the middle of them, busily inspecting the dynamite switch (which resembled a large plunger in a small box) and grumbling happily as he did so.

The Chirper had been grunting and muttering under his gag. Through his frantic chomping of his beak, he had managed to loosen the gag and was now able to blurt the odd word.

"Pertinax… glumph… sorry!" he muttered as he rubbed his beak up and down Pertinax's back. The gruff gorilla could tell that the Chirper was trying to loosen his bindings – but he kept on hitting the gorilla's ticklish spots as he did so.

"Teeheehee!" giggled Pertinax in a high-pitched squeal.

Lord Snide whirled round.

"Who was that!?" he demanded. He was met with stony silence, and a stern-faced Pertinax looking at him.

Grunting, Lord Snide turned back to inspect the switch.

"A – YOO – HOO – HOO!" squealed the laughter once more.

Lord Snide whirled round again.

"Right! Who was that?"

He could see a couple of stern-looking slyenas staring crestfallen at the ground, a mockodile holding back tears, and that strange gorilla in a chef's hat, with that bird fidgeting behind him. Silence everywhere.

If he had looked closer, he would have seen Pertinax's frown as he struggled to keep in the giggles about to erupt forth. Tears were brimming from his eyes, and his belly rippled. The Chirper kept rubbing his beak.

"Almost… there… I'm… free!" he squawked. But the last pull up of his head caught Pertinax's most ticklish spot, and the gorilla burst forth with mighty laughter.

"Pahahaha–a hoo – ahoo – ahoo!" he giggled, stamping his feet.

Lord Snide ran forward, straight at the gorilla, waggling a finger.

"Shut up! Shut up, you beast!"

Sometimes, in the most serious situations, laughter can be dangerously contagious, and it spread like a fire through the circle of animals. The frowning slyenas started sniggering, the Boogaloo let out fluffy chuckles and the mockodiles snapped in delight. Soon, there was a stamping of hooves, a clacking of beaks, and a shaking of manes – all united in glorious laughter. The Chirper, sensing that it was Pertinax's chortle driving it, kept tickling the gorilla until his giggles flew through the air.

"SHUT UP! Shut up shut up shut up – UP SHUT!" screamed Lord Snide, bouncing on the spot and causing two indentations.

"Right! That's it! I'm going to get my gun! Don't go anywhere… well… not that you can!" he snarled, and thundered off up the steps to the café. The laughter stopped – almost as quickly as it had begun.

As he waddled off, the Chirper spoke up.

"Right… we need to buy the Narzat some time. If we get up and run together, Lord Snide will have to chase us!"

"But we're all tied together," whined a spotted zebra.

"And he'll probably just threaten us if we stay put," added a dandylion.

"Besides, why risk ourselves for one little creature?" shouted a *triple-trunked mammoth*.

The Chirper, normally so jovial, so friendly, shook with rage. His feathers stood on end and his beak snapped as he spoke.

"How dare you! Shame on you all! Do you know there is one animal who never thinks like that? One animal who would never put himself first? The Narzat! " he cried. In his rage, he had managed to pull a wing loose. He pointed at each animal in turn.

"Hippo-roo – when you got wedged in that hole practising handstands, who rushed to get hug-a-slug grease to pull you out?" The hippo-roo silently muttered the word "Narzat".

"Dandylion – when you were almost eaten alive by *land piranha*, who swang in and saved you?"

The dandylion looked down.

"When your pups were trapped in a field of smallcanoes, who saved them, Slyena? The Narzat did!"

Pertinax raised his voice.

"When my chilli was too fiery, the Narzat raced off to find me some *ice-flowers* to cool my customers down!"

"He taught me how to open coconuts!" chirped a chattermonkey.

"He helped rebuild my treehouse!" croaked one voice.

"He hugged me when I cried!" growled another.

The circle became a chorus of voices, all singing of tales of bravery, and kindness, and friendship all shown by the Narzat. The Chirper raised his voice again, wriggling his other wing free to clap his hands.

"You see? And for his sake, all we need to do now is pull together!"

There was muttering and much nodding of heads.

"Um... but what should we do *exactly*?" questioned Pertinax.

"What I just said! Pull together! Everyone pull in different directions. If we all make a royal rumpus, Lord Snide won't know what to do and he'll be distracted long enough for Looky and the Narzat to hatch their plan!"

The animals nodded. Pertinax whispered in the Chirper's ear, "How do you know they'll have a plan?"

"Oh... I know the Looky Lizard. She will have a plan. Now – let's pull! PULL!"

He raised his voice and squawked, the animals straining and pulling – wriggling their arms and stamping their hooves, or flapping their wings and kicking their flippers. The wire whirred through the air – straining and stirring.

Lord Snide arrived at the Jumble Jungle Wood Café entrance, vigorously polishing his gun. He grinned evilly to himself as he unsteadily picked his large feet down the steps.

"PULL! PULL!" shrieked the Chirper.

Lord Snide looked up. The circle of animals was stretching out – pulling further and further away.

"Oh no you don't!" he bellowed, racing down the steps.

The wire strained.

Lord Snide tried aiming his gun and running down the steps at the same time. He slipped, and bounded down each stair – gaining momentum like a snowball on a mountain. With an almighty crash, he hit the bottom of the steps and rolled along the ground towards the middle of the animal circle.

"PULL! PULL!" cried the Chirper, the other animals' voices straining with him. Every muscle – every sinew – every fibre was pushing and pulling in every direction.

Lord Snide had landed, face down, some distance from his gun. But he was within a few metres of the dynamite switch. He crawled towards it.

"PULL! WE'RE ALMOST THERE!" cried the Chirper.

Lord Snide placed a hand on the switch.

An almighty sound whipped through the air.

The wire had snapped. Animals spilled outward from the circle.

Furiously, Lord Snide mashed the switch with his hand. Nothing happened.

The wire had been broken into dozens – if not hundreds – of little pieces, and the animals were now stampeding about freely.

Lord Snide rolled backwards and reached for his gun. His fingers clenched round the barrel, but a pair of hooves kicked the handle away for him. He scrambled to his feet, and his eyes met a spotted zebra. It whinnied at him and scampered off. Whirling round, Lord Snide saw the Boogaloo Bear clutching his rifle. He ran, shoulder barging into the Bear and sending it flying backwards towards the edge of the Dark Lake. As he did so, the gun flew into the air – and was snatched by a black, furry hand.

Pertinax loomed over Lord Snide. He grabbed the rifle by either end and heaved with all of his might. It snapped in half, making a loud bang as it did so. The explosion caused Pertinax to stumble backwards, leaving two shattered halves of Lord Snide's weapon on the ground.

Lord Snide looked at the swirling, whooping animals circling him. He had to get them. He had to get all of them. Turning round, his bulging eyes settled on the box of explosives. Yes! That would serve them right. Hurrying towards it, he wrenched the lid off and pulled out a large red stick of dynamite. A wire fuse curled from the top of it like a tail.

The Chirper could see what the man was doing and flapped over to him, pecking at his shins.

Lord Snide kicked the bird hard in the ribs, knocking the breath from him. He reached down and grasped the Chirper, tucking him under one arm and placing the dynamite in the bird's beak.

With his free hand, he grabbed a lighter from one pocket, and flicked it alight with his fingers. He held it above the dynamite, which was wedged firmly in the Chirper's mouth.

"Everybody stop!" he roared, "or I'll stuff this turkey and light the fuse before you know what's hit him!"

The animals froze. The Chirper gulped. Lord Snide sneered, his slobbery lips curling.

"Right! All of you – you need to shut up and do as you're told. I am man. You are nothing. I am in charge. You need to listen! You will—" his voice trailed off. The ground was trembling – no shaking – jumping even! The animals seemed to be bouncing in the air. In the distance, at the edges of the clearing, the trees were bending outwards. Lord Snide's eyes were drawn to the towering square-pear trees on the edge of the lake. The Narzat emerged, sprinting from them.

With a roar, the trees seemed to burst as a huge beast exploded from between them in a shower of bark and splinters. For Lord Snide and many of the animals, it was the first time they had ever seen the Ravenoserous. Its black and white fur bristled as its wide mouth – and rows, and rows of razor sharp teeth – spread wide. Its claws tore chunks of mud as it sprinted. No one noticed the tiny Lizard following in its wake.

"Gunarg! Gaarg!" roared the Narzat, running towards the animals and waving at them to get to safety. They clambered and leapt, sweeping from the area – clearing a path towards Lord Snide. The Narzat sprinted towards him.

The Chirper raised his head in shock, causing the dynamite in his beak to catch the flame from Lord Snide's lighter. He spat it out, and it rolled towards the box of TNT.

"Over here! Over here! Yoohoo!" he shouted.

"SHUT UP! SHUT UP!" cried Lord Snide as the Narzat, and the Ravenoserous, came closer.

"You don't want that scrap of mud do you? Look at this juicy big bird here!" cawed the Chirper.

Somewhere in the Ravenoserous' hungry mind, the Chirper's logic struck it. Its eyes swivelled from the Narzat it was chasing, and to the large man they were approaching.

Lord Snide grabbed the flaming dynamite from the floor next to him and roared back at the Narzat.

"Stop that thing coming closer or I'll blow you both up!"

The Narzat did not listen. He barrelled into Lord Snide, wrenching his friend from his arms and rolling on to the base of the steps. The Ravenoserous now stamped towards Lord Snide, who stared into its dark eyes. He noticed how the creature's eyelashes were shaped like fangs as it loomed over him.

"STOP! I command you! You filthy beasts!" roared Lord Snide. And that was the last thing he ever said.

For at that moment, the Ravenoserous lowered its head and scooped the huge man –and his box of dynamite – up with one gulp. With a vicious chewing noise, it tossed its head back and roared.

Panting with exhaustion, it turned its head and eyes to face the Narzat and the small bird in his arms, lying at the bottom of the steps. It paced forwards. The two friends were cornered.

Widening its jaws, and its ferocious eyes, the Ravenoserous reared on to its hind legs and let out a foul roar that blasted the air with fury. It did not notice the tiny green blur roll in front of it.

A tiny rock hit the beast's nose. The Ravenoserous snapped its jaws shut angrily.

The Looky Looky Lizard had placed herself between the Ravenoserous and her friends. Her scales glowed

with that brilliant blue and she rose on to her hind legs, hands raised high and her tail poised. Her eyes narrowed in anger. The Ravenoserous had taken one family from her. It would not do it again.

The monster's nose wrinkled in a cruel sneer and it padded closer, its lips trembling with fury.

The Looky Lizard placed her hands on her hips and glared. She opened her mouth as if to speak and…

BOOM!

A huge explosion – an incredible, terrible sound – blasted and it came from within the Ravenoserous' many stomachs. The dynamite!

Tears sprung to the Ravenoserous' eyes, and its belly suddenly bulged – expanding wildly and suddenly – and it released a dreadful, booming belch. If you have ever seen an adult at home eating something impossibly spicy,

you would appreciate the Ravenoserous' reaction right at this moment. The creature rolled backwards whimpering. Smoke poured out of its ears and it pawed at its tongue. Tears poured from its toothy eyes.

For a monster that had eaten many things and any things, the Ravenoserous had never experienced something like stomach ache in any of its many bellies – certainly not an ache like this. It did not understand. How had that little lizard done this? The beast turned and looked back at the Looky Lizard, bowing its head and tucking its tail between its legs.

Looky lunged forward and shook her fist.

The Ravenoserous gulped. With a final whining whimper, it turned and ran straight for the jungle, never to be seen again. Whether it was the dynamite or digesting Lord Snide, its insatiable hunger had been cured for good.

So desperate was the Ravenoserous' escape, that he even knocked over a few trees as he fled. Several koala moles clung to the roots of the upturned trees, confused as to why they'd found themselves suddenly above ground.

Looky Lizard ran up to her friends, and they wrapped their arms – and wings – round one another.

"How very sweet…" yawned a voice.

Lady Snide stood at the top of the stairs, brandishing one of Pertinax's large silver knives.

"I guess you saved me the trouble of getting rid of that big oaf," she sneered. "Narzat – bring the necklace now. Or you will never see Polly again."

She turned on her heel and vanished into the darkness of the doorway. Her voice rang out one last time.

"And come alone."

Chapter 19

The Night is Long and Dark

The Narzat crept up the stairs, his heart thundering. He walked through the doorway into the café. It all looked so different. Gone was the steady stream of laughter and gentle conversation – instead, darkness and silence flooded the room.

"Over here, beast," growled a voice.

Standing by the wide window, their backs to the Diamond Waterfall, were Lady Snide and Polly. Polly's hands remained tied behind her back. Lady Snide clutched the maid's hair with one hand, and held a silver knife to her throat with the other.

The Narzat had never been one to notice looks, but it struck him how truly hideous Lady Snide

appeared. From her
narrowed eyebrows,
to her pouting lips,
to the slicked-back
hair, every
part of her
face dripped
with malice.
Her red nails seemed
more vicious than the
claws of any beast, and
the rubies within the
sparkling tiara astride
her head glinted like
fresh blood.

"Necklace. Now,"
demanded Lady Snide.

"Don't give it to her – just run!" trembled Polly.

The Narzat shook his head. The light gleamed on
the silver knife dangerously. He slowly removed the
necklace – his shiny – and took a step forward.

"Come… put it down on the table here… That's
it… slowly!" purred Lady Snide as she directed
the Narzat. "Don't come too close – my husband

underestimated you. That was his downfall. Now – sit down."

The Narzat sat down cautiously on a rock stool. The necklace lay on the table in front of them.

Lady Snide gripped Polly's hair harder with one hand, and swept the necklace closer towards her with the knife. Her eyes narrowed as she stared at it.

"That's it. I mean… that's it?" she sneered. "That's Lady Snide's most valuable treasure?"

"Of course it is!" blurted Polly. "Her mother made it for her! And she passed it down to me. And I gave it to my son…"

Lady Snide shook her head.

"But… what's it made of? What's it worth?" she demanded.

Polly smiled.

"I don't think it's made out of any precious material… but it's made of memories. It's made with the hopes and wishes of someone who cares. It's worth everything to the person who gave it and it's worth just as much to the person who received it," smiled Polly. "I thought you knew that that's what Margaret meant when she said it was her most valuable possession!"

The Narzat nodded in agreement.

"Why would any of that matter? You mean…you mean…" shrieked Lady Snide, "that all this time – all these years – we've been looking for a plain piece of scrap metal?"

"Well… you've got it now," hushed Polly. "We can go home. The Snide fortune is yours without Lord Snide…. Just let the Narzat go first. "

Lady Snide remained frozen, her eyes staring in disbelief at the necklace. Something close to a tear brimmed in her eye. She relaxed her grip on Polly and the knife hung limply by her side. Silence ruled her features as the waterfall splashed majestically.

"Go," she growled. "Go now, Narzat, and let me leave with no trouble."

The Narzat looked across to Polly.

"Oh no," trembled Lady Snide, "Polly is staying with me. Go now and no harm will come to anyone."

She gestured with her head towards the doorway.

The Narzat reluctantly climbed to his feet and looked up at Polly. He shook his head. Polly nodded at him slowly.

"It's for the best," she trembled.

As he padded away, turning his back on the two women, Polly called after him.

"Narzat. If this is the last time I see you, please remember one thing…" she soothed. She cleared her throat and her voice rose into a melodic farewell. "Remember this… *When the night is long and dark, we fear the sun shall not rise. But – oh my friend, soon it does… and what beauty fills our eyes.*"

The Narzat froze. He knew those words. They had flooded his mind and his dreams ever since he was small – and they were always spoken in the same voice – Polly's.

The very poem awaked a memory within his heart, and he turned round.

"Grrr?" he growled delicately, taking a step forward.

"You need to go," whispered Polly. "It's the only way to keep you safe."

The Narzat took a step forward.

"Please, Narzat," hushed Polly.

"I told you to go," insisted Lady Snide, lifting her knife.

"Please!" repeated Polly. "As soon as you've gone, we'll leave."

"We'll leave," chuckled Lady Snide, cruelly. "We'll leave? As if I want to spend a second longer with *you* – you good-for-nothing goody, goody."

Polly turned and looked in confusion at Lady Snide.

"You see, I was going to wait until the Narzat was gone to do this... but it's probably more fun if he watches," Lady Snide sneered.

"I'm sorry, Polly, but I'm going to have to let you

go," she whispered. And with that, she pulled Polly backwards and pushed her through the window into the Diamond Waterfall. Polly barely had time to scream as she vanished into the water.

The Narzat froze in horror. His eyes widened and he ran to the window ledge, staring down into that horrible darkness below. Lady Snide leaned down and whispered in his ear.

"You know… she can't swim," she purred. "You can keep the necklace."

The Narzat barely heard her footsteps stamping out of the cave. A storm of fear was roaring through him. The terror of water, the horror of ever stepping foot in it – years and years of avoidance and panic and nightmares – but none of that mattered now. Only one thing did. Polly.

Blinking back his tears, the Narzat held his breath and dived headfirst into the waterfall.

***

Lady Snide snuck down the steps, brandishing the silver knife. The animals were all gathered around the Dark Lake staring in. They had heard Polly's scream as she fell, and had seen the Narzat dive after her.

Every pair of eyes was desperately peering into the water, trying to find a sign of their friends..

Lady Snide's thin red lips parted into a carnivorous smile as she tiptoed past the distracted animals and towards the treeline. As she reached there, a small voice croaked at her.

"Narzat! Narzat!"

That strange frog from earlier leapt up and down in front of her, blocking her path. She leaned forward and sneered.

"You know... you've all done me a huge favour disposing of the Snide fortune... When I return home, the Snide fortune is mine. And I'll spend it on coming back here and capturing every single one of you ... you freaks!" she shrieked.

She pointed the knife at the frog.

"Now... tell me which way my camp is or I'll dice you into pieces," she snarled.

The PhonoFrog raised a finger and pointed into the treeline. Lady Snide stormed away, hacking viciously at branches as she went.

Watching her go, the PhonoFrog felt a flicker of guilt for lying and pointing in the wrong direction... but he was fairly sure that that woman deserved it. He shrugged and bounded towards the Dark Lake.

***

Darkness. The sunlight faded fast as the Narzat kicked his legs. The coldness wrapped around him, squeezing at his chest and tearing at his muscles. His

eyes blinked rapidly in the gloom, trying to find Polly through the blur of his vision.

Nightmares of this moment – sinking in the water – swirled through his mind. Memories of crashing waves, choking water stung him as his arms thrashed. The air grew tighter and tighter in his chest. His throat ached. He needed to breathe in, he needed to breathe out but all he could do was keep swimming.

There – ahead! A shape in the gloom. It was thrashing and kicking – small bubbles of air leaving as it sank further. It had to be Polly.

The Narzat pushed through the water, his hands crawling and his feet stinging. Every sinew, every fibre ached.

His heart pounded in his ears. A pain pierced his stomach. He could see the shape now.

He was almost there... reaching out....

That's when he saw it. Like monstrous tentacles, long vines slithered from the depths below. The tales of dark weed were true. The vines slowly wound their way up and around Polly. She shook and kicked back, but they wrapped around her legs squeezing at her stomach. Her eyes closed and she wriggled and thrashed. More vines snaked their way up towards her.

The Narzat kicked his legs further still. He could feel his jaw tightening, and his eyes stung from the cold. He swam behind Polly and tried to untie her hands. His numb fingers fumbled with the knot of her apron. A strand of dark weed began to slither across his foot.

Suddenly, a hand closed around his. For that second, in the gloom and the deep, he felt a surge of warmth. Polly's arms were free. The Narzat felt the deathly cold of dark weed slime up his ankle, and he kicked his foot away. A small cry left his mouth, and bubbles floated upwards. Water rushed into his throat. His chest tightened. Darkness was closing in.

Polly tried kicking up, but the vines had all gathered round her middle, pushing her apron against her as they eagerly snatched her downwards. The Narzat held her hand, pulling with all his might – but the dark weed was stronger and now they were both being dragged down.

Polly shook her head at him. He had to let her go. He had to save himself.

The Narzat shook his head. Grasping with both hands, he heaved and pulled. Polly slipped towards him. She glanced down.

Her apron! The vines were squeezing her by her apron! She managed to wriggle her body up, out of the apron, and shiver forward. The more the dark weed gripped at it, the more she was able to pull free. The Narzat grasped and pulled and heaved and struggled and yanked and strained and… she was free!

The vines snatched the apron downwards and into the watery darkness, but more were wending their way up towards them.

Hand in hand, the Narzat and Polly began to kick upwards. They moved slowly, their muscles sore from the fight. The sunlight above them seemed as distant as a star in the night sky.

Above the surface, no one spoke. The animals had gathered round the edge of the pool in silence. TheChirper and the Looky Lizard were running up and down the bank, desperately searching for a sign of their friends. Pertinax, cradling his chef's hat in his hands found himself muttering.

"Come on you two. We believe in you."

He said it again. This time, slightly louder.

"Come on you two. We believe in you."

In the café, a few of the animals overheard him and some of them joined in.

"Come on you two. We believe in you."

Soon, other animals heard and before long the whole of the Watering Hole were chanting in unison.

"Come on you two! We believe in you!"

With whooping and stamping, and screeching and screaming, every creature was yelling

"Come on you two! We believe in you!"

Perhaps, in the darkness the Narzat and Polly could hear the chant. They kicked some more – their lungs bursting, their jaws aching. A vine snatched at their feet.

"Come on you two! We believe in you!"

Perhaps, in the darkness, it was enough. Enough to encourage them onwards.

"Come on you two! We believe in you!" the voices of every animal (and I hope whoever is reading this) boomed, wishing the pair to the surface.

For Polly and the Narzat, the light above them was so much clearer – so much closer! – but they were both growing dizzy. The Narzat's body shook, and the world was growing colder.

"Come on you two! We believe in you!"

CRASH!

The Narzat and Polly erupted out of the water – their eyes blurry from the water and blinded by the sudden sunlight after the darkness of the pool. They gasped greedily for air, scrambling on the surface of the Dark Lake.

But they did not pause for long. The vines of dark weed were still below. They kicked together, trying to get closer to the nearest bank. Gentle currents from the waterfall drove them forward to the edge.

Finally, they reached the dry land. Polly clambered out, heaving herself up on to the ground. Spluttering, she turned to face the Narzat.

He climbed out of the water, illuminated by the sunlight.

The churning waterfall had blasted away years of mud. Dirt had flooded off him through the frantic kicking, the twigs and foliage torn from his hair. Cold water had washed down his throat – clearing the remnants of shushberries. The Narzat stood in front of Polly – no longer a muddy creature.

Instead, there stood a young boy.

A young boy with golden hair and eyes of the deepest brown. Only his smile had stayed the same. With a grin, he reached out towards Polly and spoke – just one word but the most perfect word she had ever heard. Smiling, he said:

"Mum?"

Chapter 20

The Truth of It All

Lady Snide traipsed through the forest, snarling. She swished her knife at every branch that crossed her path, and a few that didn't. Cursing that damned frog, she pictured all the terrible things she would wreak upon the Jumble Jungle Wood once she had returned home. She stumbled forward and into a clearing.

It looked like a tropical beach. A large green dome lay there, fringed by sand. It slowly opened and the most beautiful flower that she had ever seen slowly unfurled and raised itself up on its stem. Taking one look at the flashing colours of its petals, Lady Snide gripped her knife closer. She had to have it.

She stepped forward, placing one foot on the sand. She stepped again. And froze. Her feet were sinking. Tugging her legs upward, she sneered at the ground. What was happening?

The flower rocked gently, as if staring at her. She tugged at her legs, and found she had sunk past her knees.

A nearby gladder slithered to the edge of the path, grinning and tilting its head to one side.

"Get off me! I demand it!" roared Lady Snide, hacking at the sand with the knife and clawing at it with her other hand. The sand had now wrapped itself around her waist.

More gladders had joined the path – some were gently knotting themselves into a rope ladder, ready to reach out to the poor woman. One of them hissed loudly.

Lady Snide shrieked.

"Eugh! What are you? You repulsive creatures!"

The snakes looked taken aback. Lady Snide pointed her knife at them.

"Yes! I said 'repulsive'! Are you as stupid as you are ugly?"

She sunk some more, but focused on yelling at the snakes.

"My God – don't you even have dentists out here?!" she growled, staring at their teeth. Several of the gladders huffed, and slithered away.

"Oi! Don't leave! Help me! I command it!" she snarled, waving her knife with her one free hand. The sand had wended itself around her neck and only her head and one arm was free. One gladder was left now, debating about what to do.

"What's wrong with you? What's wrong with all of you? Save me or I'll slash you with this knife. Do it, you vile, despicable—"

The gladder slithered away before he could hear

any more of her insults, but her voice did not last for long.

The flower rocked in the air, and – as soon as silence fell – recoiled back into its dome.

Lady Snide was gone, leaving nothing but a silver knife and a tiara full of rubies floating on the surface of the sand.

**

"They're over here! They're over here! They're safe!" bellowed Pertinax once he had found the Narzat and Polly. A stream of animals flowed towards them, encircling with praise and joy, but also taken aback by the strange new appearance of the Narzat.

The Chatty Chirper and Looky Lizard pushed in front of all of the other creatures and paused. Their friend was gone – a human stood in his place – but then he smiled that same, wonderful grin and they rushed forward to hug him.

All the time, Polly kept hold of his hand and kept on whispering to him, to anyone that would listen,

"I found him. I can't believe I found him."

The celebrations continued into the evening, when Pertinax prepared a mighty feast. His famous Jungle

Chilli was served with steaming piles of *wild garlic bread* (this was not bread made with wild garlic, but garlic bread that had grown in the wild).

Slyenas and mockodiles sat together, whilst the PhonoFrog had a wonderful time reading the menu to anyone who'd listen. Of course, Pertinax mourned the loss of his favourite knife, but someone would just tickle him if he seemed too glum. A flock of gladders slithered in and retold the tale of Lady Snide's sticky end to anyone who'd listen. Every animal tried to hide a smirk as they nodded respectfully.

But one table in particular positively boomed with

laughter and happiness. The Narzat sat talking to his mum – both staring enraptured as they gabbled and spoke about years' worth of achievements and feelings that had gone unspoken.

"That poem! That poem!" the Narzat cried, proudly sporting the necklace once again, "When you said it… that's when I knew. You were my mum, Mum."

"I used to say it to you every night, before bed," whispered Polly. "I never knew you'd remember!"

"But the thing is… sorry…. The thing is…" The Narzat paused, finding the words tasting strange in his mouth. "Sorry – it's so weird not growling and roaring…"

"That would be the shushberries!" cawed the Chatty Chirper, pausing from sipping a large bugnilla milkshake.

"What?" asked Polly.

"The shushberries – Looky has just explained to me!" he boasted proudly.

Looky, putting down a slice of wild garlic bread the size of her, climbed on to the table.

It'll be easier to show you. Let's finish eating first.

The Narzat and Polly didn't mind. They had plenty to discuss first, like how they had always dreamt of each other, what their favourite foods were, or who the Narzat had got his eyes from. Polly even told him his real name.

It was the early hours of the morning when the partying had finally stopped. After the final animal had left the party, and Pertinax had fallen asleep (headfirst in a banana cake), the Narzat, Polly, and the Chatty Chirper followed the Looky Lizard through the jungle.

The moonlight had bleached the jungle of its colour, and they seemed to be travelling through a black and white picture as they walked. Flashes of silver illuminated their path as they continued in a mixture of excited chatter and eager silence.

Finally, they arrived at the clear stream. Taking a breath, the Narzat brought himself to wade through the water to the other side. A grin of pride crossed his face as he did so.

The Looky Lizard showed them the shattered toy box, and rearranged the letters of Narzat to make Tarzan. She danced round, miming and gesturing, the Narzat translating for Polly so she could keep up with the speed of the story.

"So… as a child I must have washed up here. I would have crawled out on to the muddy bank, getting covered as I did so!" cried the Narzat. He glanced down at his legs, which were indeed covered in mud.

"The first thing I ate would be those shushberries…
which stopped me from being able to talk! And then
the PhonoFrog – YES! I remember him! – read the
letters and gave me the name 'Narzat'!"

"And, of course," interrupted the Chirper, " you
were petrified of water – probably after your hideous
sea voyage – which explains why you never washed
the mud off, or undid the work of the shushberries!"

A large thumping caught their attention. The
Looky Lizard had crawled inside the box and had
found something. She heaved and pulled out a letter
in a stamped envelope. She scurried over to Polly and
passed it to her.

"Thank you," she whispered.

"Don't mention it," chirruped the Chirper. "It's
just a letter that Looky found. She finds all sorts of
things – once she found me a rotten banana and I
tell you—"

"No," laughed Polly. "Thank you. Thank you for
looking after my boy for all these years. If there's
anything I can do for you both…" She put the letter
in her pocket, and wrapped her arms around the
Looky Lizard and the Chatty Chirper. The bird, for
once, was at a loss for words. There was one thing

his friends could do for him, but it would involve an adventure so dangerous and daring that it would need to wait for another day. Besides, right at this moment, his new family had grown again. These moments are worth savouring.

"It's almost sunrise," commented the Narzat. He pointed at a tree, "Come on!"

After a short climb, they sat high in the canopy of the tallest tree, overlooking the Jumble Jungle Wood. Dawn was beginning to flood in – the light gently beginning to colour the sky golden and fringe the clouds with pink. The sun was yet to make its entrance.

The Narzat sat, with his head resting on Polly's shoulder, with the Chirper and Looky Lizard curled up together, snoozing in their laps. Polly grasped the letter from Margaret in her hand.

"What's in the letter?" the Narzat asked sleepily.

"Oh nothing... nothing much," she murmured. "It says that we can have the necklace, and the Snide Fortune."

"The Snide fortune?"

"Yes... their house, their land, ridiculous amounts of money in the bank," she smiled.

The Narzat reached out and held Polly's hand.

"I think we're alright here, Mum," he smiled.

Her hand closed round his, and she kissed him on the forehead.

"I think we are too," she whispered.

"Besides, I've got a feeling that we're going to have plenty more adventures now you're here," chuckled the Narzat, his grin shining more than ever before.

The sun slowly began its journey over the treetops, filling the land with light as a new day began in the Jumble Jungle Wood.

And mother and son, surrounded by their friends, sat together. Their hearts smiled at the wonder of such a feeling and the joy of such a sight.

> For when the night is long and dark,
>   We fear the sun shall not rise.
> But – oh! My love – soon it does,
> And what beauty fills our eyes.